The Journey BEGINS

NIROSHA SHARMA

BLUEROSE PUBLISHERS
U.K.

Copyright © Nirosha Sharma 2025

All rights reserved by author. No part of this publication may be reproduced, stored in a retrieval system or transmitted in any form or by any means, electronic, mechanical, photocopying, recording or otherwise, without the prior permission of the author. Although every precaution has been taken to verify the accuracy of the information contained herein, the publisher assumes no responsibility for any errors or omissions. No liability is assumed for damages that may result from the use of information contained within.

BlueRose Publishers takes no responsibility for any damages, losses, or liabilities that may arise from the use or misuse of the information, products, or services provided in this publication.

For permissions requests or inquiries regarding this publication, please contact:

BLUEROSE PUBLISHERS
www.BlueRoseONE.com
info@bluerosepublishers.com
+4407342408967

ISBN: 978-93-6783-357-5

Cover design: Daksh
Typesetting: Tanya Raj Upadhyay

First Edition: February 2025

AUTHORS PAGE

Step into a world of wonder and enchantment!

Greetings! I'm Nirosha Sharma, and at just 12 years old, I'm overjoyed to unveil my debut fantasy book. Immerse yourself in a realm where every page sparkles with magic and mystery. My story is a whimsical journey through twists of revenge, heartfelt betrayals, and moments that will make you laugh and dream. With a sprinkle of fairy dust and boundless imagination, I've woven a tale that dances in fantasy and emotion. As you explore this magical adventure, it may it find its rightful place in every heart and on every bookshelf. If my story enchants you, share its magic with friends, family, and fellow dreamers. Together, let's make this spellbinding tale a global sensation!

Violet, **Amber** *and Emerald were best friends, and they used to do everything together, here is a small introduction spanning the next 12 pages.*

VIOLET

Name – Violet
Nick name –Vivo
Age –15
Birthdate –3rd may 2009
Personality - Meet violet, a 15 years old with short black hair and bangs, deep ocean blue eyes, and fair skin. She's laid-back yet deeply caring about her friends, always ready to listen and offer support. She hates alarm clocks, specially the blue one that sits on her bed side table beside her favourite lavender coloured night lamp. Violet loves animals and dreams of becoming a zoologist. On weekends, you will find her playing video games with her friends. In school, she excels in biology and art, blending her creativity with a passion for nature. Her style is unique, mixing comfort with a touch of whimsy that is reflected in her vibrant personality.

(VOILET'S DAD)
VICTOR

Name –Victor
Nick name –Vicky
Age –43
Birthdate – 14th June 1981
Job – Writer

Personality – Meet Victor, a mysterious writer with slicked-back hair, one strand gently touching the top of his cheek, glasses, and deep brown eyes that seem to hold untold secrets with a leaf tattoo on his right wrist. He enjoys seclusion, finding inspiration in his quiet home, filled with books and intriguing artwork. Victor's writing captivates readers with its mysterious charm, exploring themes that unravel secrets and leave them fascinated by the unknown.

(VIOLET'S DOG)
VANILLA

Name - Vanilla

Nick name - Ice cream

Age - 1 month

Birthdate - 3rd may

Breed - Australian shepherd

Personality - Meet Vanilla, the lively Australian Shepherd with a striking coat of blue, black and white. Known for his playful tricks and love of tearing into toys, Vanilla is a spirited companion who delights in learning new tricks. With his striking blue eyes and affectionate nature, he brings boundless joy and charm to his family's everyday adventures.

Amber

Name – Amber
Nick name – Ash
Age – 15
Birthdate – 7th April 2009
Personality – Meet Amber, a fearless redhead with a fluffy wolf cut and dazzling light hazel eyes with fair skin. She specifically hates dandelions. Polite and driven, she excels in martial arts and dreams of becoming a boxer. Amber's disciplined training and competitive spirit inspire others to pursue their dreams with courage and determination.

(Amber's mom) Audrey

Name – Audrey
Nick name - Raya
Age – 40
Birthdate – 11th April 1984
Job – police officer

Personality – Audrey is a fearless police officer known for her courage and strength. Her unwavering commitment to justice and a sharp mind makes her a respected figure in the law enforcement. Audrey's bravery and integrity inspire both her peers and the community she serves, embodying the essence of a true hero.

(Amber's dad) Andrew

Name – Andrew
Nick name – Drake
Age – 43
Birthdate – 12th July 1981
Job – Fire-fighter

Personality – Andrew is a brave fire-fighter known for his selflessness and quick thinking in the heat of the moment. His dedication to saving lives and protecting his community makes him a respected hero among colleagues and beyond.

(Amber's dog) ARMY

Name – Army
Nick name – Ace
Age – 5 years
Birthdate – 7th April
Breed – German shepherd

Personality – Army, the brave German shepherd, received a bravery award for confronting a terrorist. Known for his loyalty and fearless spirit, he embodies the true essence of a hero, dedicated to protecting others with unwavering courage.

EMERALD

Name – Emerald

Nick name – Emma

Age –15

Birthdate – 14th January 2010

Personality - Emerald is a sweet, girly girl who loves city life but is afraid of nature and wild animals. Her charm and kindness shines through, despite her fears. Emerald is defined by her long, flowing brown hair that cascades with grace, perfectly complementing her mesmerizing green eyes. Her appearance, a blend of natural beauty and sophistication, adds to her allure and charm, making her a captivating presence in any setting she embraces.

(EMERALDS MOM) ELOISE

Name – Eloise

Nick name - Eli

Age –40

Birthdate – 25th January 1984

Job – fashion designer

Personality – Eloise is a fashion designer who thrives on calmness and patience, traits that match her love for organized living and elegant fashion. She pays meticulous attention to detail, infusing her work with refined taste and creativity. Eloise's designs are a testament to her dedication, blending style and precision to create pieces that captivate and inspire.

(Emerald's dad) Edward

Name – Edward

Nick name – Eddy

Age – 43

Birthdate – 18th February 1981

Job – C.E.O

Personality: - Edward, with his brown hair and olive-green eyes, is a CEO known for his exceptional kindness and generosity. His inclusive leadership style creates a supportive environment where everyone feels valued. Edward's personal warmth and compassion make him a beloved figure both in business and his community, blending creativity with empathy to leave a positive impact on all who know him.

(Emerald's Cat)
Echo

Name – Echo

Nick name – Elf

Age – 1 year

Birthdate – 14TH January

Breed – Ragdoll

Personality – She may be lazy, but her adorable charm makes everyone love her. As a ragdoll with soft grey fur and captivating green eyes, she exudes a relaxed and laid-back vibe. Despite her laziness, she's affectionate and enjoys lounging in cosy spots, bringing comfort and joy to those around her with her gentle and easy-going nature.

Three best friends, their hearts aglow,

Step into realms where moonlight flows.

**With kindness as their compass
and courage as their guide,**

They wander through wonders where dreams softly glide.

In the weave of twilight and stardust's embrace,

Their sprits will journey through time and space.

Embrace the adventure, where magic takes wing,

For within this realm,

THE JOURNEY BEGINS.

SUMMER HOLIDAYS HAVE JUST BEGUN.

On a sunlit summer morning, Violet's heart danced with joy at the summer break's arrival. The golden sunlight promised endless freedom and adventure, painting the day in hues of excitement and possibility. Yet, as the thrill of vacation began to settle in, a shadow of sadness crept into her heart. The plans for the summer included a month-long camping trip in the Amazon jungle—an extraordinary adventure, but one that meant she would be far away from her beloved friends. The idea of leaving behind the familiarity of home and her close-knit circle of friends cast a veil of gloom over her excitement. The prospect of spending a month in the vast, untamed wilderness of the jungle felt both thrilling and daunting. Simultaneously, the separation from her friends loomed large in her mind. As the weight of this bittersweet departure began to settle in, a gentle chime from her phone drew her attention. Violet glanced at the screen to see a message from her bestie, Amber.

Hey!

Hi!

Do you want to know something exciting? We are coming to the camp with you!!!!

Really? YAY!!!!!!!!!

TABLE OF CONTENTS

CHAPTER-1 CAMP HAS JUST STARTED.......... 1

CHAPTER-2 ZOCADABRA!!!! 6

CHAPTER- 3 THE MYTH............................ 13

CHAPTER-4 THE FOX WEDDING................ 16

CHAPTER-5 THE NIGHT WALKER 23

CHAPTER-6 WHAT!? 37

CHAPTER-7 THE TRUTH 42

CHAPTER-8 THE SIREN'S NEST 66

CHAPTER-9 HEART OF THE CELESTIAL STAR 77

CHAPTER-10 THE TEAR OF THE LUNAR NIGHTINGALE 83

CHAPTER-11 PETAL OF THE ASTRAL LOTUS 89

CHAPTER-12 PHOENIX FEATHER OF THE ETERNAL FLAME 94

CHAPTER-13 THE BRACELET OF CREATION 102

CHAPTER-1
CAMP HAS JUST STARTED

On the inaugural day of the camp, the atmosphere buzzed with palpable excitement amongst all the girls as they eagerly anticipated encountering new species of animals, exotic plants, and various intriguing discoveries. Violet bought her guitar which was made out of wood and was painted in a shade of light brown. Amber bought her bass guitar as well but it was painted in a ruby red and was decorated with some cool stickers while Emerald bought her beautiful flute with her decorated with dangling crystals. A notable highlight was when Emerald, stepping out of her comfort zone, displayed newfound courage by gently touching a playful baby tiger, a moment that marked a significant personal milestone for her. As twilight descended, the setting transitioned into a cosy gathering around a crackling bonfire for the time-honored tradition of roasting marshmallows, culminating in the eagerly-awaited segment of sharing spine-chilling horror stories. The air was thick with anticipation as each camper awaited their turn to weave a tale that would send shivers down their peer's spines. As the storytelling session unfolded, it was Violet who took the lead, transporting her audience into a mysterious narrative realm. "Once upon a time, there were three adventurous young girls similar to us, venturing into the depths of the Amazon during their own camping expedition. One of the bold girls veered off the path, stumbling upon a concealed cave shrouded in shadows. Despite her fear, curiosity led her further inside, where the echoing sound of snoring combined with the eerie silence. To her astonishment, what emerged from the shadows was a sight that froze her in place..." "GIRLS" said Violet in horror, "why are you guy's snoring?" She giggled to herself and slept with her friends.

On the second day of their exciting camping expedition, Violet, Amber, and Emerald were each given specific tasks to make their camp more awesome. Violet swung her axe with gusto, gathering a mountain of firewood for a toasty campfire. Amber, with her keen eye and quick hands, scouted the trees for the juiciest fruits, dreaming of fruity snacks under the stars. Meanwhile, Emerald, meticulous as ever, piled up dry leaves, envisioning tidy campgrounds and cosy firesides. Their day was going splendidly until they realized that they had wandered off the path back to camp. *Fear crept in, even Amber's usual bravery giving way to nervousness.* But instead of letting panic take over, they joined forces, pooling their skills and creativity. Using the materials they had gathered— Violet's sturdy logs, Amber's delicious fruits, and Emerald's perfectly dry leaves—they embarked on an impromptu building project. With Violet as the chief architect, they constructed a quirky wooden shelter that wouldn't win any awards for architecture but certainly made them proud. Amber set up a makeshift picnic with the fruits, while Emerald artfully arranged the leaves for insulation, turning their shelter into a cosy one. As the sun dipped below the horizon, they snuggled inside their cosy shelter chatting about how their day went and planning how they would find their way back to camp the next day. The night air was filled with the scent of wood and the sounds of chirping crickets, a scene straight out of their favourite camping tales. Exhausted, they eventually settled into their snug shelter, finding comfort and warmth in their shared laughter. Under the vast sky scattered with twinkling stars, they drifted off to sleep, safe in the knowledge that together, they could conquer any challenge the wilderness threw at them.

The girls stirred awake all together, bathed in a brilliant light that illuminated their skin, provoking them to exclaim in unity, "AHHHHH, shine monster!" It was an inside joke among them, born from their shared adventures and unplanned humour. They burst into laughter, their voices echoing off the cave walls. As they settled into their surroundings, Emerald, always curious, broke the silence by sharing,

"Hey, you know what? I had a really particular dream last night." Almost immediately, Amber and Violet responded, "Me too!" Curiosity piqued, Emerald leaned in, eager to hear more. Violet, with a hint of grief mixed with wonder, narrated, *"It was about my grandfather. He appeared in this eerie realm, urging us to embark on a quest—to reach a lofty goal, choose the right path, solve a mystery, and ultimately save ZOCADABRA."* The name rolled off her tongue like a secret code, mysterious and captivating. Amber and Emerald exchanged doubtful glances. "OMG, no way! I had the same dream!" Amber exclaimed, her eyes wide with astonishment. The coincidence sent shivers down their spines, the lines between reality and dream blurring in the cave's dim light. Before they could delve deeper into the dream's meaning, Violet redirected their attention. "Guys, remember yesterday? We were in our cosy wood house. How did we end up in this cave?" The question hung in the air. Suddenly, as if in response to Violet's question, a bright light flooded the cave once more. Its intensity enclosed them, washing away their thoughts and leaving them stunned. Time seemed to stand still as they exchanged panicky glances and fainted.

CHAPTER-2
ZOCADABRA!!!!

A thunderous noise shattered the calmness of the jungle, startling Violet awake. "VIOLET, WAKE UP!!!" Shouted a voice that seemed to echo through the trees. Blinking in confusion, Violet rubbed her eyes and muttered, "Umm, who are you?" Before anyone could answer, a wild, energetic scream erupted from the eastern part of the jungle, "YEEHAAA". Emerald turned towards the source of the noise and found herself gazing at a breath-taking sight: a deep-green jungle, teeming with life. Towering trees swayed gracefully in the breeze, sunlight filtered through the whole jungle, and the air was filled with the sweet fragrance of tropical flowers. Emerald's jaw dropped, her eyes went wide with wonder, unable to find words to describe the beauty before her. Meanwhile, Amber was in the middle of explaining who Violet was when Emerald tapped her on the shoulder. Startled, Amber turned and gasped in amazement at the stunning view. It took her a moment to process that she was actually standing in such a magical place. Just as the trio was soaking in the mesmerizing scenery, there came a sudden crash nearby, followed by an apologetic voice muttering, "Ouch, umm, sorry about that." They turned to see a figure emerging from the dense leaves, looking slightly confused yet firm. With a touch of awkwardness, he straightened up and cleared his throat, "Uh, you can call me Hounder. Yeah, that'll do." The girls, still overwhelmed by the beauty around them, got nervous and tried to hide. The figure was still not visible but they could make out that it was definitely a human. Amber pushed the girls behind her guarding them with her arms. A tall, magical-looking man suddenly appeared before the girls in the dim cave. His hair was a messy tangle of dark strands, and his face glowed with a mysterious charm. But what really caught their attention were his eyes—one was a deep, sparkling navy blue with a bold black ring around it, and the other was a warm, twinkling hazel that seemed to wink at them mischievously. He was wearing a dark green body suit, which seemed like it was very hard and stiff, it had a light green cape with golden embroidery, the suit itself had many golden details on it. Amber, trying to keep her cool but failing spectacularly, blurted out, "Who are you? And we're not frightened, just... flabbergasted!" His lips curled into a dazzling smile as he replied smoothly, his voice tinged with amusement, "I'm Hounder, the prince of the Zocalas" his gaze sweeping over them like a playful breeze, "and you've stumbled upon my humble abode." Amber and her friends exchanged amazed looks. "Your cave?" She repeated, still trying to wrap her head around it. Hounder nodded enthusiastically. "Nope, I just hang here, Welcome to the Hideaway Hollow." Violet, both puzzled and intrigued, jumped in with a mix of wonder and disbelief, "So, did you magically bring us here, or are we just dreaming?" Amber quickly chimed in, "Yeah, we're all ears—or in your case, all eyes." Hounder chuckled, a twinkle of mischief dancing in his dual-coloured eyes. "Ah, a captive audience! Well, I didn't duck the question—" Before he could finish, a voice echoed through the cave, "Duck!" All three girls squealed and dropped to the ground as a big, friendly duck flapped its wings overhead, narrowly missing them. They peeked up from the ground, wide-eyed and giggling. Emerald, trying to be brave, asked with a grin, "Hounder, is this your pet duck? Does he quack you up?" Hounder grinned broadly. "That's Quackers!" He exclaimed, as Quackers waddled over with a comical quack. "He's quite the show-off, but don't worry, he's all feathers and no bite!" Amber raised an eyebrow, trying to sound stern but unable to suppress a smile. "Quackers?" She repeated with a giggle. "Really?" Hounder nodded, his smile infectious. "Quackers the Duck!" He confirmed with a playful wink. Violet couldn't help but shake her head in amused disbelief, a grin spreading across her face. "This is... absolutely quackers!" As they stood together in the cosy, dimly lit cave, the echoes of their laughter bounced off the stone walls and Quackers waddling around, the girls decided to trust Hounder and go with him as he was the only human they could see.

(Scene changes into a dense forest)

A man living in the forest said "Wakalalla maga ooio himo", it meant (it is coming get ready) an arrow pierced right into a flying ducks heart, "talk about a bull's eye" said the man who shot the arrow. The people who lived in Zocadabra called themselves the Zocalas. After a few hours Ohira, the king of Zocalas saw Hounder and the girls coming. He shouted, "lookala Hounder kalla" which meant (Hounder is coming with some girls). Apparently, Hounder was the only Zocala who knew 39 different languages, but all the Zocalas were not like him. Ohira also knew English and some other languages but not as many as Hounder. When they reached the tribe, everyone nervously started pushing and hitting the girls. But after Hounder said, "olicha mahala koil" which meant (they are harmless) they all got quite and stopped hitting and pushing them. At that very moment Amber saw a huge rock which was about to be thrown at them.

"STOP!!" Yelled Hounder, leaping in front of the baffled girls shielding them. "Why," muttered Ohira with a wrinkled brow, questioning Hounder's sudden protectiveness. "They are harmless!" Hounder responded emphatically, his hands gesturing vigorously to convey his assurance. Ohira, the tribe's formidable king, hesitated. His concern was real; he feared the girls might pose a threat to their community. After a brief silence, he addressed Hounder in their native tongue:

"Himikiya cha cha de ju mala himala keriya." Hounder's eyes brightened as he nodded in understanding, translating Ohira's words for the girls, "Hounder, son, you are one of us, and that's why I trust you. I'll let these girls stay with us and we'll assist them in reaching their destination." Grateful, Hounder conveyed their leader's decision to the girls, who exchanged uneasy smiles before retreating to an isolated spot, forming a circle as they debated upon their difficulty. Amber spoke first, her voice tinged with suspicion: "I don't trust this man, and their weird language gives me the creeps." Violet chimed in, echoing Amber's apprehension: "Yeah, me too! What if they're plotting against us, and we're just standing clueless?" Emerald, ever the voice of reason, countered with a glimmer of positivity: "Guys, remember, he's the one who pulled us out of that cave! Plus, we can ask them to speak in English. Besides, out there, it's a jungle—literally! We're safer sticking with them for now." After a moment of inspection, the girls reached a decision, casting uncertain glances at each other before nodding in hesitant agreement. With a collective sigh, they resigned themselves to their fate. Violet went to Hounder and questioned him, "Hounder, if you are the prince, Ohira must be your dad right?" Hounder sighed, "No, he is not, you see, before Ohira became the king, there was some other king, but the tribe did not like him, so they decided to make Ohira the king. The night before Ohira's coronation, the old king kidnapped Ohira's son and daughter, his wife passed away because of the pain and sorrow she had to go through after the incident. My mother and father devoted their life in finding Ohira's daughter and son but even after giving their whole life, the missing children were not found and nether they are now. After my mom and dad passed away, Ohira felt pity for me and adopted me as his own. He loves me as his own child. The love my mom and dad never gave me, I got it from Ohira. Violet kept her hand on Hounder's Shoulder, "It's ok, everything is going to be all right, I too don't have a mom, my dad said she passed away after giving birth to me."

CHAPTER- 3
THE MYTH

It was midnight, and the full moon bathed everything in its silvery glow. The girls were peacefully sleeping in a wooden hut crafted by the ZOCALAS tribe. Suddenly, Amber jolted awake to the sound of panicked voices shouting in the local language: "Everyone, gather around the fire quickly!" Amber quickly woke up Violet and Emerald, and they hurried outside. To their alarm, they found the tribe huddled near the blazing fire pit, looking terrified. The girls rushed to Hounder, asking frantically what was happening. Just as Hounder began to explain, Ohira interrupted sharply, his face pale with fear. "It's them!" He exclaimed, sending a chill down the girls' spines. Amber, trying to steady her voice, asked cautiously, "Who are 'them'?" Ohira's eyes widened in dread as he whispered, *"The LESHY—a shape-shifting creature. It can appear human or take the form of animals and plants. In legends, it guides travellers to safety or doom, depending on its mood."* The girls gasped in horror as they noticed a towering figure resembling a tree standing ominously behind Ohira. "Do you see it?" He asked quietly. Amber nodded slowly her eyes fixed on the eerie creature. With a sudden gasp, Amber woke up abruptly, her heart racing. She let out a relieved sigh, realizing it was just a very vivid and unsettling dream. she suddenly realized Violet and Emerald were nowhere in sight. Rushing outside, she was stunned to find the ZOCALAS tribe clustered anxiously around the blazing fire pit, just as she had dreamt. Ohira and Violet were in the middle of a heated argument, discussing a dangerous shape-shifting creature. "STOP!" Amber interrupted angrily. "What's happening here?" Violet sighed with relief. "Thank goodness you're here. Ohira's talking about some creature that can change its shape. It's ridiculous" she added. Amber's blood ran cold. She had just dreamt of the same creature, but she kept her thoughts to herself. The argument subsided, and the trio decided to explore their unfamiliar surroundings. As they ventured forth, they were greeted by bizarre sights—a bunny soaring through the air with its ears! The girls marvelled at the spectacle, but Amber felt a sense of unease creeping in. Strange scrapes and unsettling noises filled her ears, and suddenly, her surroundings seemed to drain of colour, turning an eerie grey. Grasping her head in pain, she shielded her ears from the discord. Then, in a disorienting moment, Amber caught a brief glimpse of a monstrous figure looming behind Violet and Emerald. Overwhelmed, she collapsed.

When Amber finally regained consciousness, her friends hovered anxiously around her. Her head throbbed painfully, and her vision was still blurry. Ohira, his expression grave, suddenly leaped forward, his eyes widening with an eerie smirk. "It's them," he murmured cryptically. Amber's heart sank. Her dream hadn't been just a dream—it was a terrifying glimpse into a reality they now faced.

CHAPTER-4
THE FOX WEDDING

"As I wandered through the dense forest, I was captivated by the mysterious sound of drumming echoing through the trees. Curiosity led me deeper until I stumbled upon a large gathering of foxes. Startled, I quickly hid behind a tree, observing quietly to avoid rattling them. One fox, with keen eyes, noticed my presence and signalled to the others. All the foxes snapped their fingers together and the weather around them shifted strangely: the sun continued to shine brightly, yet rain poured down heavily. I watched in awe as I realized I was witnessing a fox wedding unfold before my eyes. Despite getting soaked by the unexpected rain, I found myself spellbound by the dreamlike scene."
"This is what happened yesterday." Amber shared

the tale with Ohira. His response was unexpectedly knowing. "I knew it, it's not the leshy troubling you, it's the curse." he remarked cryptically. Confused, Amber asked what he meant. Ohira explained, "The fox wedding—it happens once a year. The foxes are clever; they trick humans into believing it's raining under a sunny sky to maintain their privacy." Amber's curiosity deepened as she wondered aloud about her recent episodes of fainting and visions. Ohira chuckled softly before launching into a traditional tale: "In Japan, there's a myth about the fox wedding. If a person glimpses it, misfortune may follow." Nervously, Amber inquired about a cure for this supposed bad luck. Ohira's expression turned thoughtful. "I'm not sure," he admitted, "but I will search for answers."

Ohira was deeply engrossed in his books, searching for a cure for Amber's mysterious illness, when Violet abruptly interrupted him. "You really should go OUT and find the cure," she urged, pushing him towards the door with determination when she realized, he had a leaf tattoo on his right wrist. She asked, "What is this?" Ohira said, "This is the tattoo given to every leader of The Zocala tribe." Violet replied, "It seems oddly familiar, but whatever, now go out!" Reluctantly, Ohira agreed. "Okay, okay," he surrendered, heading out with a sense of purpose. Recalling that the cave where Hounder had found the girls might hold answers, Ohira embarked on the tiring journey there. After what felt like an eternity, Ohira finally arrived at the cave's mouth. Stepping inside, he was instantly gripped by a chilling terror that made him scream for help. To his surprise, a mysterious figure appeared from the shadows and reassured him to calm down. "Who are you? How did you get here?" Ohira demanded, his heart still racing. The boy shrugged carelessly. "I have no idea how I got here. You are the only human I see and I've got nowhere else to go, so I guess I'll follow you," he replied casually. Thinking the girls might know him, Ohira decided to bring the boy back to the tribe. Once there, he offered the stranger some warm tea and inquired if the girls recognized him. To Ohira's surprise, they shook their heads in a no. Amber, ever curious, asked the boy his name. With a hint of mischief in his eyes, he countered, "Tell me your names first." The girls introduced themselves one by one— Violet, Amber, and Emerald.

The boy smiled faintly. "I'm... Evan. Nice to meet you," he finally offered. Evan had beautiful blue eyes just like Violet's, he had dark black, wavy hair covering most of his eye brows and he was wearing a black oversized hoodie and some grey cargos. He seemed very similar to Violet. Amber wasted no time in probing Evan about their surroundings. "Do you know anything about this place?" She inquired eagerly. Evan chuckled lightly. "Nah, why would I? I'm from Earth, which I hope this is!" He replied with a sense of humour. Ohira, sensing an opportunity, asked Evan "No this is not Earth, Its Zocadabra. And..... Do you know anything about the Myth of The Fox Wedding? From Japan?" Evan's eyes lit up with recognition. "Oh, I know about that. You get some kind of curse if you witness it, right?" Excitedly, Ohira pressed further. "Do you know its cure?" Evan nodded knowingly. "Oh yeah, I do. You just have to kill a fox." Amber's gaze bore into Evan, but before tension could rise, she burst into laughter. "You're quite the character," she exclaimed playfully. Evan grinned mischievously. "Tell me something I DON'T know." Amber, ever ready for action, with a twinkle in her eye, "Alright, who's coming with me to hunt down a fox?"

(Scene changes into the forest)

Amber, determined to lift the curse from witnessing the fox wedding, ventured deep into the forest in search of a fox to hunt. Her keen eyes spotted one almost immediately, and she silently approached him, readying her knife. With a warrior's cry, she charged towards the unsuspecting fox, committed on fulfilling her mission. But to her astonishment, the fox didn't flee in fear. Instead, it let out a shrill scream of protest. Amber slipped to a pause, puzzled. "You can talk?!" She exclaimed incredulously. The fox, clearly peeved, responded with a hint of sarcasm, "Yes, of course I can talk. But why on Zocadabra were you trying to kill me?" "I-I thought I had to" Amber stammered, her confidence wavering. "EXCUSE ME?" The fox scoffed, raising an eyebrow. Amber approached him, trying to clarify the situation. "Listen, I need to kill a fox to break a curse. And you happen to be a fox." The fox burst into hilarious laughter, startling Amber. "Wait, you what? Hahaha," it chuckled uncontrollably. Feeling a flush of embarrassment, Amber demanded, "What's so funny?" The fox composed itself, wiping away tears of laughter. "You don't have to kill a fox for that" it explained, still grinning. "Just apologize to the fox whose wedding you witnessed. He'll say a magical word, and poof! Your curse will vanish." Amber blinked in disbelief, realizing she had been on a misguided mission all along. Awkwardly, she nodded, appreciating the fox's unexpected wisdom. "Well, that would have been good to know earlier" she admitted regretfully. The fox chuckled again, its eyes twinkling mischievously. "Humans" it muttered, shaking its head. "Always jumping to conclusions, and by the way it was my wedding, I'm Felix." Amber stared at Felix doubtfully, still processing the fact that she was about to hunt down the very fox whose wedding had cursed her with bad luck. Felix, now calm but still fighting back laughter, confirmed, "Yes, it was my wedding you stumbled upon." Feeling a mix of relief and embarrassment, Amber quickly apologized, "I'm really sorry, Felix. Please, say the magical words to lift this curse!" Felix chuckled, enjoying the irony of the situation. "Alright, alright," he conceded, "the word is 'rain'. Now you're free."

Amber breathed a sigh of relief and thanked Felix sincerely. As she turned to leave, Felix called out,

"Wait! What's YOUR name?" "I'm Amber," she replied warmly, feeling a newfound kinship with the mischievous fox. "Hope we meet again, Felix." But Felix wasn't done yet. With a mischievous glint in his eye, he handed her a locket with a rain drop design on it. "Here you go," he said with a laugh, "this is for sparing my life. If you ever need me, just hold this locket and call my name. Oh, and here's the fun part," he added, barely able to contain his amusement, "if you snap your fingers while holding it, it'll rain cats and dogs!" Amber burst into laughter, appreciating Felix's unexpected gift. "Thank you, Felix," she said between giggles as she wore it, "I'll remember that." Returning to the tribe, Amber decided to spice up her adventure a bit.

When asked about her fox hunt, she timidly replied, "Oh, it was quite difficult," leaving everyone to imagine the daring adventure she had supposedly undertaken. Little did they know the truth: that Amber had not only spared a fox's life but had gained an unlikely friend and a whimsical souvenir that promised both practical help and endless amusement.

CHAPTER-5
THE NIGHT WALKER

After Evan joined the tribe, Emerald's behaviour changed drastically. She became withdrawn and distant, often lost in what seemed like terrifying dreams. Her friends noticed that she wasn't sleeping well, if at all through the night, and began to worry about her. One day, Violet couldn't hold back her concern any longer and confronted Emerald about her behaviour. "Emerald, what's been going on with you lately?" She demanded, her frustration evident. Emerald, normally quiet, leaned in close and whispered, "My dreams... they're so scary. I keep dreaming that we're trapped here forever and ever." Violet's expression softened with empathy. "We need to talk to Ohira," she decided. Approaching Ohira with urgency, Violet described

Emerald's distressing dreams and asked for an explanation. Ohira's face darkened as he anticipated the situation. "There's only one explanation: The Night Walker, or the Dream Controller," he murmured sternly. Confused, Emerald asked, "Why would he be giving me these nightmares?" "You'll have to ask him yourself," Ohira replied sombrely. "Alone." Determined to confront her fears, Emerald inquired, "How do I reach him?" Ohira took out an ancient, worn-out book and flipped through its pages until he found what he was looking for. "Ah, here it is," he said, pointing to a section about The Night Walker. "First, you must journey to the Black Mountains, where you'll face your deepest fear. If you overcome this, you'll travel through a vast desert to reach the Kingdom of the Clouds, where your wisdom and strength will be tested. Finally, if you pass these trials, you'll be taken to the Kingdom of Dreams, where you can find The Night Walker and can ask him anything." Emerald's determination hardened. She announced to everyone that she would depart for the Kingdom of Dreams the next day. Ohira tore a page from the book, handing Emerald a map and the essentials for her journey. "Take care," he advised soberly. As Emerald prepared to embark on her quest, the tribe watched with a mixture of worry and hope, knowing she was about to face challenges that would test her courage and determination like never before. Violet and Amber helped Emerald pack her backpack for the journey ahead. Violet couldn't hide her worry. "Are you sure you don't want us to come with you? I'm really concerned," she fretted. Emerald reassured them with a smile, "Don't worry, girls. I'll be fine. Come here." The three friends embraced tightly, but emotions overflowed, and Violet started crying. "The girl who's scared of dogs is off to the Kingdom of Dreams," she sniffled between sobs. The silliness of the situation made everyone laugh through their tears as Emerald set off on her journey. After traveling a mile, Emerald encountered a dying flower unlike any she had seen before—it was pitch black. Feeling sorry for it, she carefully uprooted the flower and replanted it under the shade of a large, fertile tree. She poured water from her bottle onto the flower, and to her astonishment, its colour transformed from pitch black to a stunning golden hue that emitted a brilliant light. Suddenly, a gentle voice echoed in her mind, "Hello, pretty girl. I am the soul of the flower. Thank you for saving me." The flower offered Emerald one of its petals, explaining that it produced a powerful light which might prove useful in the dark Black Mountain region. Emerald's eyes widened with wonder and gratitude as she accepted the shimmering golden petal. With a proud smile, she continued on her journey. Another mile later, Emerald stood before the foreboding Black Mountains. Remembering the flower's advice, she retrieved the golden petal from her bag. With a loud exclamation, she held it up, and the petal illuminated the entire area, banishing the darkness and revealing the path ahead. Excitedly exploring the region, Emerald stumbled upon a cave whose interior glowed brightly. Fascinated, she decided to enter, unaware that this decision would lead to her greatest challenge yet. As she stepped inside the cave, the walls around her transformed into a maze of mirrors, reflecting her every move with eerie precision. At first intrigued, then unsettled by the countless reflections staring back at her, she felt a chill creep down her spine. The air felt heavier, the silence punctuated only by her racing heartbeat. Confusion quickly gave way to panic as she realized each mirrored path led to another confusing twist.

Arrows painted on some mirrors pointed left, others right, and some appeared to loop back on themselves. It was a maze designed to disorient and trap. Her disguise of bravery cracked under the pressure of the puzzling reflections. Outwardly patient but inwardly trembling like a startled animal in the night, she struggled to find an escape. The mirrors seemed to multiply, distorting reality with each passing moment. Within the chaos, she noticed a peculiar sight—a mirror where her reflection wore a sinister smile, its eyes glinting with wicked intent. Intrigued and desperate for direction, she cautiously approached. The smile deepened as her reflection whispered urgently,

"RUN!" The command echoed through her mind as she sprinted down one corridor after another. Yet, with each turn, her reflections multiplied, mocking her with laughter and repeating the ominous whisper. Panic gripped her as she realized the maze was playing tricks on her mind. In a moment of clarity, she spotted a hammer encased in glass with a faded sign that read 'only use in emergency.' Without hesitation, driven by fear and determination, she shattered the glass and swung the hammer at the mirrors. Each impact shattered the illusions, but one mirror remained untouched, its surface ominously still. Approaching it cautiously, her reflection began to speak with a chilling certainty, "It's not over ye—" With a primal scream, she brought the hammer down with all her might, shattering the mirror into a thousand fragments. Breathing heavily, she stood amidst the remains, declaring fiercely, "It's over". Relief rushed through her as she burst from the maze, only to find herself confronted by a vast, barren desert under a blazing sun. The stark transition from fear to freedom turned her delight into uncertainty, as she faced the intimidating expanse ahead. Exhausted and thirsty, Emerald dragged herself forward, every step being a struggle in the ruthless desert heat. Just when she thought she couldn't go on, a strange sound caught her attention—a gentle patter of falling water. Her thirst drew her towards it, and as she approached, her eyes widened in disbelief. There, cascading gracefully down a rocky formation, was a mesmerizing waterfall. She wasted no time in cupping her hands to drink. The water was cool and refreshing, soothing her dry throat. For a brief moment, she closed her eyes in gratitude, savouring the relief it brought. But as she opened her eyes, a horrifying realization dawned upon her. Instead of the lush water she had imagined, she found herself surrounded by sand. It coated her body, filled her mouth, and clung to her face. Overwhelmed by frustration and despair, a tear escaped her eye, and she collapsed to her knees, letting out a gut-wrenching scream. Hours passed before she regained consciousness. The desert had transformed under the cloak of night, the sky above a breath-taking tapestry of stars. Emerald, humbled by the beauty she had momentarily forgotten, whispered to herself, "Living in the city made me forget the true magnificence of the night." Filled with newfound courage from the celestial spectacle above, she pressed on through the eerie desert, directionless yet determined. The night deepened, and the stars seemed to shine even brighter, casting a mystical glow over the endless sands. She felt as though she could reach out and touch the entire Milky Way spread out before her. But then, just as she thought she had seen everything the desert could offer, her eyes caught sight of something unimaginable—a staircase leading skyward, its steps floating independently in mid-air.

Fashioned from luminous white marble that gleamed like the stars themselves, it defied all logic. "Is this a dream?" She whispered, hardly daring to believe what she saw. Hesitantly, she placed her foot on the first step, which instantly transformed into a vibrant shade of blue, radiating a melodious note that vibrated through the stillness of the night. As she climbed, her torn clothes miraculously transformed into a flowing white gown, its fabric soft as silk. Her long, straight brown hair flowed elegantly over her shoulders, complementing the fragile beauty of the staircase and the serene desert landscape below. Each step she took brought her closer to the top, where the staircase seemed to lead into the very heart of the starlit sky. Finally reaching the summit, she beheld it in all its glory— The Kingdom of Clouds. Below her stretched a realm of pure white clouds, illuminated by moonlight and shimmering with an otherworldly radiance. Towers and peaks of cloud stuff rose majestically, casting soft shadows under the moons watchful gaze. The air was crisp and refreshing, carrying with it the faintest hint of a melody that seemed to harmonize with the heavens above. Overwhelmed by the beauty and serenity surrounding her, Emerald realised she was somewhere extraordinary—a place where dreams met reality and the boundaries between the ordinary and the magical blurred into insignificance. Under the shimmering moonlight, Emerald stood in awe of the Kingdom of Clouds, where everyone adorned themselves in ethereal pearly white dresses with hints of iridescent colours. Men and women alike wore elegant attire, embodying a serene beauty that mirrored the serene surroundings. Among the dreamlike scene, a melodious voice called out her name, "You must be Emerald." Startled yet curious, Emerald turned to see a princess with eyes as deep as the ocean and hair as dark as the night sky—Princess Moon. Her fair skin seemed to radiate like the moon itself. "Yes, I am Emerald," she replied, captivated by the princess's presence. "And who might you be?" "I am Princess Moon," she answered with a gentle smile. "Night Walker informed me of your arrival." Excitement bubbled within Emerald. "You know Night Walker? Where can I meet him?" Moon chuckled softly, her cheeks tinged with a blush. "First, let's complete your test, and then you can meet him." Emerald couldn't help but admire Moon's beauty. "You're incredibly beautiful." "Thank you," Moon replied graciously.

Moon then began to recount a tale of friendship turned into bitter rivalry. "Long ago, the Sun and I were inseparable friends. We shared everything, but as humans began to compare us—our duration, usefulness, and more—the rivalry grew. Each time, the Sun emerged victorious. Now, I've had enough. I cannot defeat the Sun alone, but with your help, we can conquer him. Then, I will control the human world. If you assist me in destroying the Sun, I will grant you a meeting with the Night Walker." Emerald stood in disbelief, her mind whirling from Princess Moon's startling request. "Wait a minute, WHAT!" She exclaimed, unable to understand the significance of the situation. "You want me to do what?" Moon's expression remained serious as she said, "You heard me." Struck by concern, Emerald voiced her uncertainties. "Moon, this isn't right. If the Sun disappears, there will be no light on Earth, no life. And you were wrong about humans always choosing the Sun over you. Yes, the Sun is powerful, but in beauty and peace, you shine brighter. People find hope and inspiration in you. Without the Sun, there would be no comparison, no balance." She paused, her resolve firm. "I won't help you, whether you let me meet the Night Walker or not." There was a moment of tense silence before Moon seemed to reconsider. "You're right," she admitted quietly. "If the Sun is gone, life on Earth would suffer." She turned to her guard and gave a swift command. "Take Emerald to meet the Night Walker." Emerald was baffled. "But what about my test?" "This was your test," Moon explained calmly. With a snap of her fingers, she welcomed a radiant figure, glowing with a warm and bright yellow aura that seemed to spring from his very being. His tall figure exuded liveliness, with clear and sun-kissed skin. His hair, a rich brown with golden highlights, framed his face in waves. His eyes, hazel and lively, sparkled with warmth that matched the glow surrounding him. He moved with a fluid grace, casting gentle rays of light that danced across the white marble staircase and the curling clouds. His attire, simple yet elegant, shimmered as if woven from sunlight itself, reflecting his majestic and life-giving presence in the cosmic realm. He greeted Emerald kindly. Moon said with a soft smile on her face, "The Sun and I were best friends, are best friends, and will be best friends." Feeling a mix of relief and amusement, Emerald couldn't help but laugh nervously. "So, you made up this whole story just to test me?" "Yep,"

Sun chimed in, his bright behaviour contagious. "Now, where will I meet the Night Walker?" Emerald asked eagerly, ready to move past the extravagant test. "Follow me," Moon said with a mischievous glint in her eye, leading Emerald towards the KINGDOM OF DREAMS. "Finally, I get to meet the Nightwalker," exclaimed Emerald with a mix of anticipation and relief as she and Moon approached the foreboding castle with its imposing black walls. Moon, still curious about Emerald's intentions, asked again, "But why do you want to meet the Nightwalker?" Emerald hesitated for a moment, her mind racing with thoughts of the wish she sought. "I'll explain everything later," she replied, *while grinning from ear to ear.* As they approached the gate Emerald asked Moon to leave as she wanted to meet the Nightwalker alone. Moon left suspiciously. Inside, the atmosphere was thick with an ancient, mystical energy that seemed to fill every stone and corridor. The walls of the grand hall were indeed painted in deep black hues, contrasting sharply with the faint glimmers of magical blue lights that danced irregularly throughout the air. Emerald's heart pounded as she caught sight of him—the Nightwalker. He stood tall and commanding, his presence radiating an air of puzzling power. His attire was as mysterious as his reputation: a long navy-blue top hat adorned with small, twinkling white stars, a matching tailcoat with the same celestial pattern, and a long black cane that he leaned upon with a quiet confidence. His black gloves added to his mystique, contrasting sharply with his starlit style. "Nightwalker," Emerald bowed while smirking, her voice tinged with a mixture of nervousness and mischief. The Nightwalker regarded her with piercing eyes that seemed to see through her very soul. *"What do you seek from me, Emerald? And why did you LIE about having scary dreams?"* His voice was deep and booming, carrying a weight of centuries-old wisdom. Emerald took a steadying breath, knowing she had to choose her words carefully. "I seek a wish," she began, her gaze unwavering. "But I wish for a gift that I can carry with me, a wish I may use when the time is right."

The Nightwalker nodded thoughtfully, as if weighing her request against the fabric of destiny itself. Without a word, he retrieved a brooch from within the folds of his coat. It was a gorgeous piece, complexly designed with arcane symbols that seemed to shimmer faintly in the dim light of the hall. With deliberate grace, the Nightwalker began an ancient incantation, his hands moving in a mesmerizing dance around the brooch. The air around them grew thick with magic, swirling in shades of deep blue that throbbed with unseen power. "There you go," the Nightwalker chanted somberly, handing the brooch to Emerald. "This brooch contains a single wish, a manifestation of your deepest desire. Break it when you are ready, and the wish will be granted." Emerald accepted the brooch with respect, feeling the weight of its potential in her palm. She looked up at the Nightwalker with gratitude shining in her eyes. "Thank you," she whispered sincerely, knowing that this gift would shape the course of her future. With the brooch safely secured, Emerald bid farewell to the Nightwalker and began her journey back to her tribe, her heart soaring with a newfound sense of purpose and possibility. She knew that the brooch held the key to her dreams yet she also felt bad for lying to her companions.

CHAPTER-6
WHAT!?

"It's been three weeks since Emerald left," Violet confessed to Amber, her worry intense. "She said it'd only take five days. I'm starting to get really concerned." Just then, Hounder burst into the room, his face tense with urgency. "Guys, there was a landslide nearby!" Violet's anxiety spiked. "Is everyone okay?" Amber tried to reassure her. "I'm sure they'll manage. Let's stay positive." Before the tension could settle, Evan appeared with a suggestion. "Hey, girls, Ohira's about to tell us a fascinating story about this place. Wanna join?" Eventually, the tribe gathered around the crackling fire, curiosity replacing their worries. Ohira began, "Long ago, in Zocadabra, it's said there were four bracelets: Creation, Manipulation, Illusion, and

Destruction. Only the creator, and each king of the tribe, including me has seen them, and the creator alone made them. Legends claim that whoever possesses all four bracelets gains ultimate power." As the story unfolded, Violet leaned over to Hounder. "I'm really worried about Emerald." Hounder nodded gravely. "Me too." After the tale, Violet, Amber, Hounder, Ohira, and Evan gathered together. Evan broached the subject on everyone's mind. "So, where do you think Emerald is? It's been three weeks and a day since she set off." Hounder hesitated, stuttering slightly. "I-I think she might be..." Amber cut him off gently. "Let's not speculate." "Everything will be alright," Amber declared, though her voice wavered with uncertainty. "I hope so," she whispered to herself, her own fears beginning to surface. Tears streamed down Violet's cheeks as she whispered, "Let's go find her." Her voice trembled with a fear she had never known. Hounder hugged her, gently stroking her cheeks, "Don't worry we will find her." At midnight, the tribe emerged with lanterns aglow, scattering into the forest. They searched tirelessly, every shadow and valley packed with desperate hope. Hours passed in finding Emerald. By 3 AM, exhaustion blunted their resolve, and the forest remained stubbornly silent. A heart-breaking announcement confirmed their worst fears:

Emerald was declared **dead**. Violet and Amber collapsed in shared sorrow, the weight of guilt crushing them. That night stretched into eternity as tears mingled with whispered memories. Days turned into weeks, then months, without Emerald's return. Amber noticed Violet's withdrawal, her spirit dimmed by grief. One day, Amber found Violet clutching a soggy photograph, tears marking its edges. "We can't keep going on like this," Amber said gently, sitting beside her. Violet looked up, eyes filled with sadness and longing. "I miss her so much," she whispered. "We all do," Amber murmured, offering comfort. Amber wrapped Violet's Guitar around her neck and started strumming the guitar, she played a gentle tune which bought back a lot of memories. Together, they sat in the soft tune of the guitar, bound by shared loss and memories of their beloved friend. One night, Evan slipped away unnoticed from the tribe. When morning came, a note was discovered inside Evan's hut. It read: "Hello, my dear friends. I understand your concern, but I assure you, I'll be fine. I know Emerald is gone, but there's something calling me. I'll return in a few months. I want to give you all an advice. Please, don't trust me. Yours always, Evan." "No no no no, I can't lose you too. I just can't," Violet cried, her voice breaking. She fled toward the riverside, tears streaming down her cheeks. Amber hurried after her, finding Violet seated on a deck overlooking the soothing water. They sat together, legs dangling over the edge, lost in their sorrow. For a brief moment, the world seemed still. Then, the crunch of leaves behind them shattered the silence. Amber spun around, alert. Hounder approached them quietly, his voice gentle yet firm. "I know you're sad, but we need to stay strong." As if in response to his words, a piercing screech split the air, sending chills down their spines. The sound reverberated through the dense jungle, unsettling and threatening. "What was that?" Violet stammered, fear tightening her grip. A sense of dread settled over them as they realized they were not alone. They scanned their surroundings anxiously, aware that danger lurked nearby, hidden in the shadows of the jungle. "Shhh" said Hounder hushing the girls. "What is it?" Whispered Amber. Under the sunlight in the forest, Violet, Hounder, and Amber came face-to-face with a terrifying creature that emerged from the shadows. The creature attacked quickly, slashing its claws through the air. Violet dodged out of the way just in time. Hounder grabbed a thick vine and swung it hard, wrapping it around the creature's legs to slow it down. Hounder picked a sharp stone from the ground and sliced the creatures leg, a green liquid oozed out of its limb. As it did, many small insects rushed to his leg, and started to suck his blood which made him weaker and paler. Amber grabbed a sturdy branch and hit the creature hard on its side. Their plan worked. With the creature off balance, Violet and Hounder pushed it back, and Amber struck it on the head with the branch. The creature let out a loud roar of pain and frustration before retreating into the darkness and disappearing. Violet, Hounder, and Amber stood together, catching their breath. They knew they had faced a dangerous enemy and won through quick thinking and teamwork in the sunlit forest. "A-HA, you thought you could kill us? Say that to my stone," said Hounder flipping the stone in the air, and accidentally hitting himself in the head. "Ouch," said Hounder embarrassed and rubbing his head. The silent and thrilling atmosphere filled with laughter after watching what Hounder did.

TRUTH

CHAPTER-7
THE TRUTH

Weeks later, Violet was taking a relaxing walk when Amber called out to her excitedly, "Vivo, come see what we found!" Startled, Violet hurried over to where Amber and Hounder had gathered. They had discovered a note that read:

RIOHA SI A RILA!

"Someone sent this using a flying rabbit," Amber said, her voice tinged with suspicion. "What does it mean?" Violet asked, puzzled. "I'm not sure," Amber replied, studying the note from different angles. "It looks like it's written in our Zocadabarian language," said

Violet, confidently. "Nope, if you look at it, it's written in roman script but the letters seem jumbled. This 'A' here, 'R' there, and 'I' here." said Amber breaking her confidence "Let's try to decode it," Violet suggested, handing Amber a piece of paper and a pencil.

Amber carefully transcribed the sentence and experimented with rearranging the words in various ways. Eventually, she wrote the letters in such a way that it spelled out, "OHIRA IS A LIAR!" Gasping in disbelief, Violet exclaimed, "What? Who sent this to us?

What does it mean?" "I'm not sure," Amber admitted, her brow gathering with concern.

"But we should be cautious." Later that evening, Violet was thinking about the unsettling note as she strolled through the jungle. Suddenly, Hounder appeared before her, startling her out of her thoughts. "I know you're worried about the note," Hounder said sincerely, "but I want you to know that Ohira is trustworthy." "I never doubted Ohira," Violet responded softly.

"But think about it—among all of us in the jungle, only a few can write in English: you, me, Amber,

Emerald, Evan, and Ohira. It wasn't me, you, Amber, or Ohira who wrote that note. Emerald and Evan have vanished, so it couldn't have been them. That leaves no one else." Hounder nodded solemnly, understanding the seriousness of the situation. They shared a moment of concern, realizing they were facing an unknown threat within their close-knit group. As Violet and Hounder stood in thoughtful silence, the weight of the mysterious note hung heavy between them. The realization that someone among their small group might be sheltering doubts or secrets cast a shadow over their trust and friendship. "We need to figure out who could have written this," Violet said, her voice tinged with concern. "It's unsettling to think that someone might be trying to spread discord among us."Hounder nodded thoughtfully. "You're right. We've been through so much together. It's hard to believe that one of us would betray that trust." Amber approached them, sensing their unease. "Did you figure out what the note meant?" Violet hesitated, debating how much to reveal. "It spelled out 'Ohira is a liar' when decoded. But I don't believe it. Ohira has always been trustworthy." Amber frowned, her brow furrowed in deep thought.

"So, if it wasn't Ohira, then who could it be?" The trio exchanged troubled glances, grappling with the unsettling possibility of betrayal within their tight-knit group. Each face reflected a mix of loyalty and suspicion, unsure of whom they could fully trust. "We should confront Ohira about this," Hounder suggested cautiously. "Maybe there's a misunderstanding or someone is trying to frame him." Violet nodded in agreement. "Yes, we owe it to Ohira to hear his side of the story. But we must proceed carefully. Whoever wrote that note wants to create doubt and division amongst us." With a solemn resolve, they decided to seek out Ohira and confront him gently but directly. As Violet, Hounder, and Amber approached Ohira's abode in the dense jungle, they found him sitting near a flickering fire, his usual calm character tinged with surprise and confusion as they presented the mysterious note to him. Ohira looked up, his eyes widening slightly as he read the accusatory words scrawled on the paper. "OHIRA IS A LIAR!" His brow furrowed deeply, and he seemed genuinely taken back. "I... I don't understand," Ohira stammered, his voice betraying a mix of confusion and concern. "Who would write such a thing? Why would anyone think this of me?" Amber stepped forward gently, holding out the note. "We don't know, Ohira. That's why we're here. We trust you, but we need to understand what's happening."Violet nodded in agreement, her expression sympathetic yet firm. "We're not accusing you, Ohira. We just need your help to figure this out." Hounder, usually calm, shifted uneasily on his feet. "Yeah, Ohira. This note has us all on edge. We need to get to the bottom of it." Ohira took a deep breath, visibly gathering himself. "I swear to you, I have no idea who could have written this or why. I've always been honest with all of you." The tension in the air was intense as they exchanged uncertain glances. "We believe you, Ohira," Amber said softly, placing a reassuring hand on his shoulder. "But someone among us is trying to cause trouble. We need to stay united and find out who." With renewed determination, they resolved to investigate and unnoticeably, their bond strengthened by their collective resolve to uncover the truth and protect their community from discord and suspicion. Ohira, visibly shaken yet determined, joined them in their quest, his trust in his friends unwavering despite the unsettling accusation against him. "Before figuring out who wrote this, we need to find our friends" said Violet, she added, "They could help us." Suddenly Without warning, Evan emerged from the shadows, his presence sending a chill through the air. His typically warm smile was replaced by an unsettling smirk, one that sent a shiver down everyone's spine. "Well, well, well," Evan drawled, his voice laced with an eerie calmness. "What do we have here?" Violet, Amber, and Hounder turned to face Evan, their expressions a mixture of surprise and anxiety. Evan's appearance was different— there was a calculated edge to his every move, a darkness that hadn't been there before. But what caught their attention the most were the three bracelets gleaming on his wrist— bracelets they recognized from Ohira's story about Zocadabra. "Evan..." Amber began cautiously, her voice wavering slightly. "What are you doing here? And where have you been?" Evan chuckled darkly, his eyes flickering with a strange intensity as he gazed at Ohira. "Oh, just taking care of a few things, you know," he replied cryptically. "As for where I've been... let's just say I've been busy." Hounder stepped forward, his voice tinged with concern. "Evan, did you write that note, 'OHIRA IS A LIAR!'?" Evan's smirk widened into a malicious grin. "Ah, you found my little message, did you? Clever, aren't you?" Violet felt a knot tighten in her stomach as she exchanged worried glances with her friends. Evan's transformation was upsetting—they had always trusted him, but now he seemed like a different person entirely. "Ohira," Evan continued, his gaze locking onto Ohira's with an unsettling intensity. "You thought you could keep the truth hidden, didn't you? But you can't hide from me." Ohira's confusion turned to guarded realization, his eyes narrowing slightly as he judged Evan's demeanor. "Evan, what are you talking about?" Evan's grin turned chillingly cold. "You and I both know the power of these bracelets," he said, holding up his wrist to display the three gleaming artifacts. "And we both know what they can do in the wrong hands." Amber gasped softly, her eyes widening in realization "You took them," she whispered, her voice barely audible. Evan nodded slowly, his eyes glittering with triumph and malice. "Yes, I took them. And now, I have the power to do whatever I want." Violet's heart sank as she realized the depth of Evan's betrayal. He hadn't just deceived them; he had secretly stolen powerful artifacts while pretending to be one of them. "Now,"

Evan said threateningly, advancing towards Ohira and the others, "let's see how you handle the truth." He raised his hand, the bracelets glowing ominously, ready to unleash their power. Suddenly, Amber exclaimed, "They don't have their full power!" Evan stopped, turning to Amber with a chilling smile. "How? In the legend, there were four bracelets," Amber explained, her grin widening, "but you only have three. Only someone with all four can unleash the ultimate power." "That's true," Evan admitted, his smirk unwavering. "But I can still use their power separately." Amber tried to shake his confidence. "Even so, you won't win. You're alone, and we're a team." Evan's laughter reverberated around them, cold and unyielding. "Oh, I'm not alone." Suddenly, a figure emerged from the shadows, instantly recognized by Violet. A chill ran down her spine as she gasped, "Emerald?" Her voice cracked with disbelief and deep-seated hurt. Emerald stepped forward, her expression unreadable, eyes locked on Violet. The jungle spun around Violet as panic clawed at her chest, squeezing the breath from her lungs. She stumbled back, a wave of dizziness washing over her. Everything seemed strange, like a nightmare unfolding before her eyes. The silence thickened, the weight of betrayal hanging deeply between them. The revelation cut deeper than Violet could have ever imagined, shredding their trust to its core. She struggled to steady herself, but her legs felt like they might give way beneath her. Now, the room crackled with tension, a tangled web of alliances and betrayals spinning around Evan, who wielded stolen power. With a former ally now standing against them, the stakes were higher than ever. Evan's arrogance and ambition had set them on an irreversible collision course. Amidst the chaos, Violet fought to regain her composure, knowing they had to find a way to confront not only Evan's stolen power but also the fractures tearing their once-united group apart. As Violet struggled to steady herself amidst the overwhelming betrayal and tension, she felt her chest tighten with each panicked breath. The jungle swirled around her, the faces of her friends and the looming figures of Evan and Emerald blurring together into a nightmarish display. "Evan... how could you?" She managed to choke out, her voice trembling with disbelief and pain. Her gaze flickered between Evan's smug expression and Emerald's unreadable stare, her mind whirling with the enormity of their betrayal.

Evan's laughter sliced through the air like a knife. "Oh, Violet," he scoffed, revelling in her chaos. "You were always too trusting, too naive to see the truth." The accusation hit her like a physical blow, intensifying the disaster within her. The sense of betrayal cut deep, not just from Evan's actions but from Emerald's unexpected loyalty to him. She had trusted them both, believed in their shared goals, and now everything lay shattered at her feet. Amber's voice cut through the tension, firm and determined. "Violet, we need to focus. We can't let them tear us apart." Her words were a lifeline amidst the chaos, grounding Violet momentarily in the present. Blinking back tears, Violet clenched her fists, toughening herself against the panic threatening to overwhelm her. She couldn't afford to fall apart now, not when everything they had fought for hung in the balance. She forced herself to breathe deeply, to find that core of strength buried beneath the hurt and confusion. With a shaky resolve, Violet straightened, meeting Evan's gaze with newfound determination. "You may have stolen power, Evan, but you haven't won yet. We are still a team, and together we will find a way to stop you."

Evan's smirk faltered slightly, his confidence momentarily shaken by Violet's disobedience. He glanced at Emerald, a silent exchange passing between them, before he adjusted his shoulders and raised his hand again, the bracelets glowing with rehabilitated wickedness. As tensions intensified and battle lines were drawn, Violet knew that they faced their greatest challenge yet. The future hung in unwarranted balance, but she refused to let fear paralyze her. With her friends by her side, she would fight to reclaim not just the artifacts of power, but their shattered trust and unity. The stakes had never been higher, but neither had their determination to conquer against the darkness threatening to consume them all. Just as the bracelets were about to shoot, Amidst the swirling chaos, Emerald's hand shot out, grasping Evan's wrist with a determined strength. Without a word, she neatly snatched the bracelet of creation from him, her appearance was very different, her once freely flowing hair was now hastily tied up in a bun, her elegant dress swapped for a sleek, practical bodysuit that spoke of readiness and resolve. A heavy sigh escaped Emerald's lips before she spoke, her voice carrying both sadness and newfound opinion. "You've always underestimated me, believing I could do nothing without you. But now, I hold the power to reshape everything. I could create something so devastating it could bring you all to your knees in minutes." Before Emerald could act on her threatening words, Amber stepped forward, her voice trembling with a mix of fear and pleading. "Emerald, please, we don't need to do this. We can still find a way to resolve this peacefully—" Violet, sensing the intensifying tension, moved swiftly to interfere. She reached for Emerald's hand, attempting to disarm her of the bracelet. But Emerald's grip was firm, and in the struggle, the bracelet shattered into pieces that scattered across the ground. The moment hung heavy in the air, each character's stance and expression betraying their inner confusion and conflicting loyalties. Emerald's transformation from seeming weakness to an embodiment of formidable power had shifted the dynamics of their group irreversibly. The fate of their world now riskily balanced on the knife-edge of their choices and actions to come. As the shattered pieces of the bracelets lay below their feet, they all started to panic and sweat, all of them turned pale because they did not know what will happen if the bracelet of the creation breaks. The shattered pieces of the bracelet lay scattered at their feet, a blunt reminder of the irreversible moment that had just unfolded in front of their eyes. Panic and uncertainty gripped each member of the group, their faces drained of color as they exchanged worried glances. None of them had anticipated what would happen if the bracelet of creation were to break. Amber's hands trembled as she stared down at the remains, her mind racing with fear and regret. "No" she whispered, barely audible, her voice cracking under the weight of realization. "We weren't supposed to break it." Violet, usually calm and composed, looked on with wide eyes, her thoughts racing to grasp the consequences of their actions. "What have we done?" She murmured, her voice filled with disbelief. "The bracelet... it held immense power. We don't know what breaking it might unleash." Just as the group stood amidst the shattered remnants of the bracelet, grappling with the consequences of their actions, the ground beneath them began to tremble violently. A deep, threatening rumbling echoed through the jungle, sending shockwaves of fear and confusion through their already unsettled minds. Before they could react, the earth split open with an ear-splitting roar. A sharp tear tore through the dry land, gaping wide enough to swallow them whole. Hounder, Emerald, Evan, Amber, and Violet had mere seconds to react as they stumbled and fell into the gaping jaws of the earth. They tumbled through the darkness, wreckage and dust swirling around them, until they landed with a vibrating thud in an underground cave. The ground shook once more, causing loose sand and rocks to fall down from above, sealing the crack through which they had fallen. Coughing and disoriented, they picked themselves up from the sandy floor, their surroundings dimly lit by the faint glow of glowing fungi clinging to the walls. The air was thick with silence, broken only by their ragged breaths and the distant echoes of the collapse above. Amber was the first to speak, her voice echoing softly in the hollow space. "Is everyone okay?" She asked, her concern real as she checked each of her companions for injuries. Violet nodded, her eyes scanning their surroundings cautiously. "I think so," she replied, her voice tinged with unease. "But where are we? And how do we get out?" Emerald, usually quick to assert herself, was uncharacteristically quiet, her mind still reeling from the events that had emerged. She glanced around the cave, a mixture of determination and apprehension flickering in her eyes. Evan brushed off the dust from his clothes, his mind racing as he searched for a solution. "We've got to find a way out of here," he said firmly, his voice cutting through the uncertainty that hung in the air. But his words seemed to fall on deaf ears. It was Violet who suddenly grasped the severity of the situation and leaned in to for urgent whisper to Amber and Hounder, "We're stuck here unless Evan use those bracelets to break through that stone wall." Amber hesitated, clearly conflicted. "I really don't want to talk to him," she murmured under her breath. Violet continued, her voice low but insistent. "Let's focus on getting out first. We can sort everything else out later, okay?" After a moment's hesitation, Amber reluctantly nodded in agreement. Meanwhile, Hounder approached Evan, his hand gently resting on Evan's shoulder. "Hey buddy, why are you doing this? Where did things go wrong?" Evan let out a heavy sigh, his eyes revealing a mix of determination and defenseless. "Violet, Amber, do you remember me?" "Remember you?" Violet asked, a furrow forming between her brows. "Remember how we used to play together?" Evan's eyes flickered with a hint of nostalgia. "We were best friends when we were kids. My mom worked at your house, Violet. But then your dad kicked us out, and we had to move away. That's where I found these bracelets." "In my house?" Violet echoed, her voice tinged with surprise. "Yeah," Evan continued. "After that, you three became inseparable and forgot all about me. I've been alone ever since. Then, years later, when I heard you went missing on a trip to the Amazon, I went to investigate and ended up here. Ohira told me about the power of these bracelets, and I used them for revenge. But now, I just want all of us to make it home, safe." The group exchanged glances, the weight of Evan's confession sinking in. The tense atmosphere softened slightly as they began to understand the depth of Evan's loneliness and the desperation that had driven his actions. "We need to figure out a way to escape," Violet finally said, her voice gentle yet determined. "Together." Suddenly, a vivid memory surged through Violet's mind like a bolt of lightning, illuminating the dim breaks of her memory. "Violet, please don't forget me," Evan had pleaded years ago, tears glistening in his eyes." "I promise, Evan, I won't forget," Violet had vowed, her young voice tinged with both sadness and determination. In the present moment, it was as if a veil had been lifted. Violet's eyes widened with realization. "Evan, I remember you now. It's like our memories together were erased." Evan's face lit up with a mix of hope and disbelief as Violet instinctively wrapped her arms around him. The embrace was a powerful reunion, filled with emotions that had been buried deep within. Amber, moved by the heartfelt scene unfolding before her, couldn't help but join in, setting aside her initial reservations. The trio of childhood friends stood together, their bond repaired amidst the uncertainty of their surroundings. Meanwhile, Emerald stood apart, arms crossed tightly against her chest. Her heart wrestled with conflicting emotions – pride in her independence and a pang of longing for the connection she saw blossoming among her friends. As they stood united, the air around them seemed to soften, carrying with it the weight of years spent apart and the promise of settlement. "We need to find a way out of here," Evan declared, his voice steady and determined. He gently broke the embrace but kept a reassuring hand on Violet's shoulder. "Together." Violet nodded firmly, her eyes bright with newfound clarity and resolve. "Together," she echoed softly, a gentle smile of understanding playing on her lips. With Emerald remaining on the fringes, unsure whether to join or remain aloof, the group formed a circle of unity. They shared a common purpose now – to escape the imprisonment and perhaps heal the wounds of their past. In the face of the challenges ahead, they knew their strength lay not only in the mystical power of the bracelets that had brought them together but also in the enduring bonds of friendship they were rediscovering along the way. Hounder smiled softly at Evan's hesitation before turning to him with a hopeful expression. "Evan, can you use the bracelets to break through the wall?" Evan bit his lip, weighing their options. "I'll give it a shot," he finally agreed, his voice tinged with uncertainty. Focusing on the bracelet adorned with intricate symbols of illusion, Evan closed his eyes and concentrated. He envisioned a tough hammer emerging in his grasp, ready to shatter the solid stone obstructing their path. However, as the illusion took form, it unexpectedly transformed into a lone sock—a baffling sight, lacking of its pair. Before anyone could react, the sock vanished into thin air after a mere two seconds, leaving the group momentarily speechless. "Well, that didn't quite go as planned," Amber remarked humorously, breaking the stunned silence that followed. With their immediate escape plan foiled, they found themselves standing at a crossroads, uncertain of which path to take next. The walls of the cave gleamed with dampness, and the echoes of their footsteps reverberated eerily through the tunnels. Hounder took the lead, his expression now serious but resolute. "Let's explore further and see where these caves lead us," he suggested, his voice carrying a note of determination. Violet nodded in agreement, her eyes scanning their surroundings with a mix of curiosity and apprehension. "We have to find another way out," she reassured the group, her tone firm and unwavering. Emerald, still grappling with the unexpected turn of events, reluctantly fell into step behind them, her arms crossed as she silently considered their difficulty. Her conflicted emotions lingered, torn between the desire to distance herself and the indisputable pull of the friendship regenerating among her companions. As they ventured deeper into the complex passages, the air grew cooler, and no signs of light so they decide to change their path, again. This was the only way left, so it should be the right one, thought everyone. As Evan, Violet, Amber, Emerald and Hounder walked deeper into the cave, their footsteps echoed softly against the stone walls. "It's hard to believe we're the ones who broke the Bracelet of Creation." Violet murmured, breaking the silence that hung between them. Amber nodded in agreement, her voice tinged with regret. "Yeah, it's a lot to take in." Hounder, always practical, spoke up after a moment of reflection. "Well, what's done is done. Right now, we need to focus on finding our way out of here and figuring out our next steps." Evan nodded considerately, his mind swirling with thoughts of the shattered artifact and its effects. "You're right, Hounder. Let's concentrate on getting out of this cave first." Their footsteps continued to echo softly as they walked deeper into the cave. Conversation turned naturally to the topic of the missing fourth bracelet. "Do you think anyone knows where the fourth bracelet might be?" Amber wondered aloud, her voice breaking the silence. Evan considered her question carefully. "It's hard to say. The legends are unclear about its location. It could be hidden somewhere significant." Violet, scanning their surroundings, added, "Or maybe it's lost in a place no one has thought to look." Hounder nodded, his gaze flickering around the cave walls. "Don't you remember, Ohira said someone stole it, and strangely Evan found it at your house, Violet." Violet quickly defended herself, "Yeah, but years ago." Their conversation continued as they navigated the twists and turns of the cave, the occasional drip of water scattering their thoughts. Each of them wondered silently where the fourth bracelet, of Destruction might be, but they knew their instant concern was finding a way out. "We need to stay focused," Evan said, his voice breaking through the quiet hum of their thoughts. "There might be others who know about the bracelets. We can't risk anyone finding them before we do." Amber nodded, her expression determined. "Agreed. Let's keep our eyes open and stay together." With renewed resolve, they pressed forward through the tangled passages. The path ahead remained uncertain, but then, they saw a light emerging from the cave's mouth. Violet, Amber, Hounder, and Evan were immediately engulfed by the vastness of the surroundings. Towering blades of grass swayed rhythmically in the gentle breeze, their tips brushing against the explorers' legs like whispers from a giant's realm. Above them, the sky was alive with the incessant buzzing of oversized insects darting up and down, reminding them of the massive scale of this strange world that they had stumbled upon. As they tried to make sense of their surreal surroundings, a shadow fell over them. Looking up, they beheld a huge owl descending from the sky. Its wingspan seemed to stretch beyond understanding, and its eyes gleamed with ancient wisdom as it landed gracefully before them. "Welcome, travellers" the owl's voice vibrated deeply, almost shaking the ground beneath them. "What brings you to the land of giants?" "We need to make the Bracelet of Creation," Amber spoke up, her voice wavering slightly in the presence of the majestic creature. "Can you guide us on how to create it?" The owl nodded knowingly, its gaze sweeping over each of them. "Ah, the Bracelet of Creation," it rumbled thoughtfully. "To fashion such a potent artifact, you must gather rare and wondrous treasures." "What treasures do we need?" Hounder asked eagerly, his eyes wide with curiosity. The owl paused, feathers rustling as it considered the question. The owl's eyes twinkled with ancient wisdom. "To create the Bracelet of Creation, you must gather five extraordinarily rare and magical items, each embodying the essence of creation:

1 Heart of the Celestial Star: A pulsating, radiant gem containing the raw essence of a dying star. Its surface shimmers with swirling cosmic light and heat, radiating the power of celestial birth and decay.

2 Tear of the lunar Nightingale: An iridescent tear from a mythical nightingale that sings only under the light of a full moon. This tear shimmers with the light of countless stars and holds the power of celestial harmony and profound inspiration.

3 Petal of the Astral Lotus: A single, glowing petal from a mythical lotus that blooms once every thousand years. The petal radiates with the pure essence of cosmic energy and is instilled with a soft, magical glow.

4 Phoenix Feather of the Eternal Flame: A single, radiant feather from a phoenix, a legendary bird known for its rebirth from its own ashes. This feather glows with an intense, fiery light and holds the magic of renewal and eternal fire."

The owl's eyes grew serious as it spoke. "To bind these treasures together and create the Bracelet of Creation, you will need one final, essential item: "The Crimson Clasp." "It's a rare and powerful artefact," the owl explained. "To get it, you must journey to the very dangerous Siren's Nest. This nest is a place full of enchantments and traps, hidden deep within an unfaithful sea. The Crimson Clasp was once worn by the Siren Queen herself, and it holds the special magic needed to unite the powers of the other treasures you've gathered. Without it, you won't be able to complete the bracelet." The owl continued, its voice carrying a note of urgency. "Once you have the Crimson Clasp, your quest is not yet complete. You must then seek out Breeze, the Queen of Fairies. She is the only one with the power to unite all these items and create the Bracelet of Creation." Violet said filled with confidence, "come on guys, we have our tasks set ahead, let's make are way to the Siren's nest"

CHAPTER-8
THE SIREN'S NEST

To reach the Siren's Nest from the Forest of Whispers, Violet, Amber, Evan, and Hounder had to navigate a dark and twisted forest filled with eerie enchantments. The journey began deep in the forest, where the trees loomed like ancient giants and the air was thick with an unsettling magic. "Stick together and keep your wits about you," Violet said, pushing aside thick vines and branches. "This place is known for playing tricks on people." As they ventured deeper, an unexpected fog rolled in, thick and choking. It hung in the air like a living cloak, swirling and shifting. The fog wasn't naturally dense; it seemed to have a mind of its own, wrapping around them and muffling their sounds. "This fog feels alive," Evan said, straining to see through the dense mist that seemed to pulse and breathe. "We need to stay close, or we might get completely lost." The fog carried with it a chorus of whispers, faint and distorted. The voices seemed to come from nowhere and everywhere, muttering fragments of unsettling phrases and dark secrets. The whispers echoed and twisted through the fog, creating a sense of creeping fear. "What are those sounds?" Amber asked, her voice trembling as a low, somber wail drifted through the trees. The sound was both haunting and sorrowful, making the forest seem even more ominous. . Suddenly, the ground beneath their feet began to shift and twist. It felt as though the earth was alive, rolling and rolling like a giant, breathing creature. The surface sprung and flung, threatening to pull them into its depths. Hounder growled frantically, trying to keep his footing on the unstable ground. "We need to move!" Violet shouted as the ground seemed to ripple and sway, creating the illusion of a living, breathing landscape. "This place is trying to swallow us!" As they fought to stay upright, the trees around them began to twist and morph. The bark of the trees twisted into weird faces with hollow, staring eyes. The branches stretched out like clawed hands, reaching for them with an almost wicked intent. The forest seemed to come alive with cruel intent, shifting and twisting to confuse and scare them. The faces in the trees whispered cruel and mocking words, their voices blending with the haunting wails in a discord of dread. "Follow the glowing symbols!" Emerald's voice cut through the chaos. "They'll lead us out of this nightmare." Emerald led them to a stone circle partially buried in the shifting ground. The stones were covered in symbols that glowed with a sickly, beating light. The symbols seemed to move and twist, changing shape and direction as if they were alive. "These symbols are our guide," Emerald said, her voice steady despite the chaos around them. "We need to read their patterns to find our way." As they followed the glowing symbols, the forest seemed to become even more surreal. The fog parted to reveal horrifying visions: nightmarish versions of themselves with twisted features, weird creatures lurking in the shadows, and landscapes that disobeyed the laws of nature. The forest's magic blurred the line between reality and nightmare, making it nearly impossible to tell what was real. "Is this real?" Amber asked, her voice shaking as she saw a nightmarish version of herself grinning from the shadows. The vision seemed to mock her, its eyes glinting with nasty joy. "Don't look at the illusions!" Violet urged, trying to keep her focus on the symbols. "Just follow the path and ignore the visions." With great effort, they pushed through the trippy and disorienting landscape. The shifting ground eventually settled, and the weird faces and twisted branches receded. They found themselves at the base of a sheer cliff overlooking the ocean, the fog and eerie visions fading into the distance. "This is it," Evan said, looking out at the dark, churning sea. "We need to get down to that beach before the tide comes in." At the base of the cliff, they discovered a quiet, rocky beach where Emerald was waiting, looking relieved but anxious. "I'm glad you made it," Emerald said, her voice carrying a hint of urgency. "We need to move quickly. The tide is coming back in soon." Amber turned to Emerald, filled with ego but she also felt bad for her. As the low tide came, the entrance was marked by an ancient, partially submerged stone structure. The stones were coated with barnacles and seaweed, their surfaces worn smooth by the passage of time. "This is the gateway to the Siren's Nest," Emerald explained. "We need to be quick and prepared." With their enchanted breathing devices secured, the group took a deep breath and plunged into the cold, dark sea. The water was chilling and murky, and the underwater path to the Siren's Nest was mired with its own dangers. As they inclined into the depths, they braced themselves for the unknown challenges that awaited them in the eerie and deceitful world below. Once Violet, Amber, Evan, Hounder, and Emerald plunged into the cold, murky waters, they entered a nightmarish realm beneath the sea. The entrance to the Siren's Nest was an enormous, jagged archway partially obscured by thick, rotting kelp that seemed to struggle and pulse with a sickly, greenish light. Emerald pointed toward the archway with a trembling hand, signaling the group to advance. As they swam through the outlandish entrance, their movements were slow and cautious. Inside, the cavern was vast and disorienting. The walls were slick with a dark, viscous slime that seemed to breathe and shift as if alive. The dim, sickly glow from bioluminescent fungi and algae cast eerie, distorted shadows that danced and flickered on the walls.

The haunting, melodic voices of the sirens echoed faintly through the water, their eerie harmonies weaving in and out of the oppressive darkness. Amber's face knotted in disgust as she waved her hand in front of her nose, then pointed to the walls with a sweeping motion, indicating the grim surroundings. The sirens' voices seemed to swell and shift with the eerie environment, their harmonies both enchanting and unsettling. The cavern floor was covered with a twisting, jellylike mass of sea creatures that squirmed and pulsed with a disgusting, greenish light. Strange, round growths emerged from the slime, their surfaces dotted with needle-like spines. The creatures produced sickening splashes as they shifted. Evan lifted his hands in a "no touch" motion and hopped lightly to avoid stepping on the gooey mass, then looked around anxiously, making wide gestures to express his concern about navigating through the mess. The siren's voices grew slightly louder and harsher, adding to the disorienting atmosphere. Emerald examined the chamber and spotted a narrow, twisting passage partially hidden by a tangle of rotting seaweed. The seaweed was thick with a foul-smelling, black mucus that clung to their suits. Emerald pointed towards the passage with a frown, then made a signal for everyone to follow, alerting them to be slow with a gesture of her open hands. As they pushed through the rotting seaweed, it squished and dripped with thick, black fluid that oozed out in clumps. The passage was narrow and claustrophobic, with walls lined with jagged, razor-sharp coral that scraped against their suits. Violet clasped her hands over her chest, shuddering, and made small "shaking" motions with her hands to express her anxiety about the cramped conditions. The siren's haunting voices bled through the walls, their melodies weaving an unsettling tapestry of sound that echoed eerily in the confined space. Emerging from the passage, they entered a more terrifying chamber. The floor was covered with a squirming, pulsating mass of sticky organisms, which emitted a faint, unsettling glow. Their uneven and frantic movement added to the oppressive atmosphere. The chamber was filled with towering columns of twisted, weird crystal formations encrusted with thick layers of slime and fungal growth. The crystals emitted a low-frequency hum that seemed to vibrate through the water and unsettle all of them to their very core. The sirens' voices now swelled, their melodies almost seeming to taunt as if aware of their presence. In the center of the chamber stood a lavish base, covered in a thick layer of rotting seaweed. The stand was partially hidden beneath the foul, twisting mass, with the Crimson Clasp glowing with a dark, malevolent light. The siren's voices grew louder, their haunting harmonies becoming more insistent and harsher. Suddenly, the water around them began to swirl violently. A shadowy form emerged from the murky depths. As it approached, it became clear that a siren had arrived. The siren was a mesmerizing yet terrifying sight. Her elongated, twisting tail was covered in iridescent scales that shimmered with an unsettling mix of greens and blues, shifting colors with every movement. Her upper body was that of a slender woman, but her skin had a pale, almost translucent quality, giving her a ghostly appearance. Her hair flowed like tendrils of seaweed, drifting in the water as if alive. Her eyes glowed with a haunting, hypnotic light, deep and black with iridescent flecks that seemed to draw in light. Her lips were slightly parted, revealing sharp, needle-like teeth that glistened threateningly. The siren's voice was both haunting and beautiful, but it carried an underlying menace. As she sang, her voice wove a hypnotic, harmonious melody that twisted through the water like a touchable force. The eerie music seemed to pull at their senses, creating a disorienting atmosphere. Amber's eyes widened in horror as she pointed to the emerging siren, her fingers trembling. She made frantic gestures to indicate the approaching danger, while Violet's hands flew to her mouth in shock. Emerald, with a firm resolve, swam toward the base. She gestured to the rotting seaweed with a disgusted look, then pointed to the clasp, indicating her intention to retrieve it. As she reached the base, she carefully began to push aside the rotting seaweed. The seaweed seemed to resist her efforts, its black mucus oozing and clinging stubbornly. The siren's song grew more intense and hypnotic, as if trying to pull them into a trance. The gummy mass on the floor began to churn violently, reacting to her presence. The mass of creatures twisted and squirmed more frantically, and the sticky floor began to bubble and fizz. The siren's voice rose to a frantic, unmusical climax, blending with the unsettling noises of the creatures around them. The chamber seemed to pulse with a sinister energy. Emerald's hands struggled to clear the seaweed, which seemed to shift and writhe as if alive. Every time she thought she was making progress, the mass would react violently, sending a wave of muck and smut falling over her. The siren's voice became a chaotic increase, adding to the overwhelming pressure of the situation. The chamber began to shake, and the crystalline columns started to crack and shatter, sending sharp shards of crystal flying through the water. With a final, desperate effort, Emerald managed to retrieve the Crimson Clasp from the base. As she pulled it free, the entire chamber seemed to shake, with the gelatinous floor bubbling and frothing uncontrollably. The siren's song reached a frenetic, almost frenzied peak, blending with the sound of the collapsing chamber. Emerald raised her arms and waved them to signal urgency, then pointed to the surrounding area as the chamber started to collapse. Violet pointed urgently toward the narrow passage, making quick, sweeping motions with her hands to signal the need for a speedy escape. The group fought their way back through the narrow passage, navigating the rotting seaweed and slimy walls with careful, deliberate movements. The sirens' voices echoed and warbled around them, their melodies a disorienting mix of fear and allure as they hurriedly retreated. The water outside was turbulent, and the path back to the cove was fraught with danger. The haunting melodies of the sirens filled the water once more, their voices a harsh chorus that seemed to chase them as they struggled against the swirling currents. Violet's hand gestures showed the need to fight the currents, while Amber and Evan used wide, forceful motions to push against the water. The sirens' singing grew fainter but still lingered in the background, their eerie notes a reminder of the danger they had narrowly escaped. Finally, they reached the cave and emerged from the water, gasping for fresh air. They collapsed onto the shore, their bodies shaking from exhaustion and the leftovers of their traumatic experience. The Crimson Clasp was safely in their possession, but the nightmarish journey through the underwater cavern and the terrifying encounter with the siren had left them with intense, unsettling memories. Violet and Amber's gestures of relief and exhaustion were apparent as they rested, while Evan and Emerald exchanged exhausted nods, acknowledging their shared suffering. The haunting echoes of the sirens' voices still lingered in their minds, a chilling reminder of the dark depths they had survived.

CHAPTER-9
HEART OF THE CELESTIAL STAR

Emerald handed the crimson clasp to Violet and said, "Keep this safe, we shall make our way to find the heart of the celestial star within a few hours." With the clasp secure, the adventurers stepped into the forest, which was alive with magic. The trees were tall and silver, the leaves sparkling as though brushed with stardust. The air shimmered with a soft, golden light, and bioluminescent flowers bloomed along the path, their colours changing in rhythm with the clasp's gentle glow. As they ventured deeper, the forest became even more fantastical. The ground was covered in a soft, glowing moss that pulsed with a heartbeat-like rhythm. Tiny, magical creatures fluttered around them, leaving trails of shimmering dust. The fragrance in the air was sweet, like moonlit honey mixed with fresh rain. They soon discovered a whimsical village consisting of mushroom houses. These houses were enormous, with caps that resembled large, colourful umbrellas. The mushroom stems were patterned with complicated designs, and warm light spilled from their windows, creating a cozy, inviting glow. The mushroom houses swayed gently as if alive, and fairy lights floated around, adding to the enchantment. The village was full of life with activity. Little beings with delicate wings and pointed ears darted about, their laughter mingling with the magical hum of the forest. They wore garments made from leaves and gossamer, and their eyes sparkled with joy and curiosity. The mushroom houses seemed to respond to the tiny beings, shifting slightly as they moved past. As the group wandered through this magical village, an elegant elf emerged from behind a large mushroom cap. The elf wore a flowing robe that shimmered like liquid moonlight, and its eyes sparkled with ancient wisdom. It approached with a serene smile. "Greetings, travellers," the elf said, its voice soft and musical. "I am Alwen, guardian of this enchanted realm. Few have the honour of visiting our village nestled in the heart of the forest's magic." Alwen stood tall and graceful, their presence radiating a serene elegance. They had long, flowing hair the colour of moonlight, cascading in soft waves down its back. Their eyes were large and almond-shaped, a deep, mesmerizing shade of green that seemed to reflect the forest's own vibrant hues. Their skin had a delicate, almost translucent quality, with a subtle shimmer that caught the light. The elf was adorned in a robe made of shimmering fabric that seemed to blend seamlessly with the surrounding magic. The robe was a rich, deep blue, speckled with silver threads that sparkled like a night sky. The sleeves of the robe flowed gracefully with every movement, and the edge of the robe was embroidered with intricate patterns of stars and celestial symbols. Alwen's pointed ears, a signature of their fragile heritage, peeked out from their hair, adding to the ethereal appearance. Amber stepped forward and nodded respectfully. "We are looking for the Heart of the Celestial Star. We were guided here by this clasp." Alwen's gaze fell upon the clasp, and their eyes widened with recognition. "Ah, the Crimson Clasp. It is a key to the deeper mysteries of this realm. Follow the path through the village, but be wary of illusions. Trust in your hearts and the clasp's magic." With a graceful sweep of hand, Alwen indicated a path of radiant light that appeared before them. The path wove through the mushroom village, revealing its wonders. The mushroom houses, with their large, colourful caps shifted gently with the breeze, and their windows glowed warmly, casting a soft, inviting light. The houses were adorned with delicate vines and flowers that twinkled like stars, enhancing their magical ambiance. As they walked, the adventurers passed whimsical creatures—tiny fairies with glittering wings and small, mischievous gnomes darting in and out of sight. "These Animals and plants are incredible! Nothing like the ones on Earth!" Violet said, her zoologist side peeking out. The village was a living dream, each moment filled with enchantment and wonder. The path led them to a serene lake. The water's surface was perfectly smooth, mirroring the starlit sky above. As they approached, the surface began to shimmer and part, revealing a pathway of glowing stones that stretched across the lake. Each stone emitted a soft, warm light, guiding them forward. On reaching the far side, they entered a grand celestial chamber. The room was bathed in a soft, radiant light, with walls covered in floating constellations that shifted and danced. The floor was an assortment of glowing celestial symbols, each one shining with vibrant colours. At the centre of the chamber floated the Heart of the Celestial Star, a glowing orb of pure energy that bathed the room in a calming light. Violet approached the Heart with awe and admiration. As her fingers touched the orb, the entire chamber erupted in a dazzling display of light and colour. The Heart's energy mingled with the clasps, creating a harmonious glow that filled the space with beauty. The magic wrapped around them, infusing them with a profound sense of peace and clarity. As their task was completed, the celestial chamber and the mushroom village began to gently fade. The magical lights and ethereal surroundings gradually disappeared, and the familiar forest reappeared around them. The night sky above was a brilliant tapestry of stars, reflecting the celestial magic they had just experienced. The only thing which did not fade was 'The heart of the celestial star.' Violet, took out the Crimson clasp and kept the heart of the celestial star in it which just melted into the clasp, making the Clasp shinier than before. As the last of the celestial magic dissolved, the adventurers found themselves back in the familiar forest. The magical village and the grand chamber had faded, leaving only the softly glowing path and the gentle rustling of the forest around them. The air was cool and crisp, and the stars above seemed to shine even more brightly, as if the universe itself was acknowledging their extraordinary journey. Alwen's final words echoed softly in their minds. The path through the village and across the lake had been a breath-taking passage into a world beyond their wildest imaginings. Now, the forest felt calm and serene, but it was with a lingering sense of the magic they had just witnessed. "Let's sleep now, tomorrow we have to make our way to get 'The tear of the lunar nightingale'" said Emerald.

CHAPTER-10
THE TEAR OF THE LUNAR NIGHTINGALE

As the first light of dawn kissed the ancient trees of Zocadabra Forest, the world awoke in a magical symphony of gold and green. Sunbeams wove through the dense foliage, painting the forest floor in a soft, shimmering glow. Emerald, Evan, Violet, Amber, and their committed companion Hounder stirred from their restful slumber beneath a cozy blanket of moss and leaves. The forest itself seemed to stretch and sigh, as if it too was waking from a deep, enchanted dream. Emerald unrolled the ancient map with a humble touch. The parchment was adorned with delicate symbols and softly glowing lines, whispering secrets of ages past. "Our journey begins," she said softly, her voice as soothing as the morning breeze. "We must navigate these mystical woods and reach the heart of the forest by twilight. There, we will find the Lunar Nightingale and collect the Tear of the Lunar Nightingale." Violet, her short black hair ruffled and her deep ocean blue eyes still dreamy with sleep, gazed at the map with wide-eyed wonder. "We need to follow the signs—ancient trees with twisted branches, majestic rock formations, and a hidden grove." Evan, balancing a flaky protein bar while trying to untangle his shoelaces, grinned with mischievous charm. "Sounds like an epic quest! I've always wanted to face challenges like avoiding enchanted roots and keeping clear of cheeky forest nymphs." Hounder, his harsh stylishness perfectly in tune with the wild beauty of the forest, took the lead. The forest around them drummed with magic and mystery. Evan entertained them with larger-than-life tales of mythical creatures. "And then I told the dragon, if you think I'm scared, just wait until you see me deal with a squirrel manipulating a tiny sword!" Violet, her love for nature evident, paused to admire a cluster of flowers that glowed softly with a light of their own. "Look at these blooms! They only appear once every blue moon. Almost as rare as Evan's sense of direction." Amber laughed, her voice a melodic ripple through the trees. "Let's hope none of these magical plants decide to join our quest. We don't need any extra... vegetation." By afternoon, the forest revealed a grand, circular glade bathed in an ethereal light. At its center stood an ancient stone arch, adorned with runes that sparkled with a celestial shimmer. Evan struck a dramatic pose. "Behold, the Arch of Wonders! Or as I like to call it, 'The Gateway to Our Next Adventure.'" Emerald approached the arch with peaceful focus. "This matches perfectly with the map's guidance. We need to align ourselves with the moon's light to reveal the path." Violet adjusted the map with gentle care. "Let's hope there are no more surprises—like a pit of enchanted marshmallows." Evan's eyes widened in mock horror. "Marshmallows?! That's my ultimate weakness!" As the full moon began its ascent, its silver light bathed the runes in a soft, ethereal glow. With playful comments about "moon magic and cosmic adventures," they activated the device. The stone panel slid open with a whisper, revealing a passage lit by moonlight. The passage led them deeper into the forest's heart, the air growing cooler and more still. Their footsteps blended with the gentle murmur of ancient enchantments. Evan continued to entertain them with whimsical impressions of fantastical beings. At the end of the passage lay a chamber of breathtaking beauty. Crystalline formations adorned the walls, their surfaces catching the moonlight and scattering it in a dance of radiant colors. At the chamber's center stood a grand podium bathed in silvery light. Upon it was the Tear of the Lunar Nightingale, its light reflecting the brilliance of countless stars. Emerald's eyes widened in awe, but her attention was drawn to a delicate, melodious song drifting through the chamber. Amidst the shimmering crystals perched a Lunar Nightingale, its feathers iridescent and glowing with celestial light. The bird was singing softly, its voice blending with the gentle hum of the moonlit chamber. Evan, captivated by the sight, approached slowly. "Wow, it's the real Lunar Nightingale! And look at that tear—it's as radiant as the night sky!" Violet's gaze softened with wonder. "It's even more beautiful than I imagined. We must approach with care and respect." Amber, her eyes wide with admiration, added, "We've found it. Now we need to collect the Tear without disturbing the Nightingale." Emerald stepped forward, her movements graceful and deliberate. "Thank you for guiding us, noble Nightingale. We seek the Tear to honour its beauty and magic." The Lunar Nightingale tilted its head and sang a soft, harmonious note. As if understanding their determined, it fluttered gracefully to a nearby branch, allowing Emerald to gently collect the Tear. The moment Emerald touched the Tear, a warm, soothing glow encircled the chamber. The Tear's light filled them with a deep sense of unity and accomplishment. The Lunar Nightingale's song rose to a melody of celestial harmony that resonated with the forest itself. With the Tear of the Lunar Nightingale secured, they turned to leave the chamber. As they emerged from the passage and stepped into the moonlit clearing, the forest greeted them with a tranquil, silver embrace. Violet, then added the tear into the Crimson clasp, and again, the tear merely dissolved. Just then, a soft, melodious chirping caught their attention. Among the forest's shimmering undergrowth, a tiny, magical baby bird had just hatched. Its feathers glowed with a soft, iridescent sheen, reflecting the moonlight like a constellation of tiny stars. The bird flapped its delicate wings and chirped a sweet, enchanting tune. Evan, enchanted by the sight, bent down with a wide smile. "Look at that! A baby bird, fresh from its magical egg. How adorable!" Violet's eyes sparkled with affection. "It looks like it's taken a liking to us. We should take care of it." Amber, her voice warm and delighted, added, "It seems to have chosen us as its new friends. Perhaps it's a sign of good fortune." Evan gently cradled the baby bird in his hands. "How about we name it Silver? It seems perfect." "Silver it is," Violet agreed, her heart full of warmth. "Welcome to the team, Silver!" With Silver nestled comfortably on Evan's shoulder, the group made their way out of the forest. The moonlight danced around them, casting a serene, silver glow as they walked. The forest, now alive with their achievement, seemed to whisper its blessings. Now, with their squad complete, nothing could stop them in accomplishing their goals.

CHAPTER-11
PETAL OF THE ASTRAL LOTUS

In the mystical forest of Zocadabra, five fifteen-year-olds—Violet, Emerald, Amber, Evan, Silver and Hounder—were on a critical quest to restore the shattered Bracelet of Creation. Having successfully retrieved three of the six magical items, they now sought the fourth: the Petal of the Astral Lotus. The forest was a magical wonderland, vibrant with shifting lights and mystical creatures. Violet, who dreamed of becoming a zoologist, was especially thrilled by the forest's enchanting wildlife. Emerald, though less fond of nature, was determined to see the quest through. Evan, with his deep knowledge of ancient lore, was cracking the magical map. Amber, practical and watchful, kept an eye out for any threats. Hounder, their clever and resourceful friend, used his keen mind and strategic thinking to help navigate the challenges ahead. As they trekked through the forest, Violet couldn't hide her excitement. "This place is amazing! Look at all these magical creatures!" Emerald sighed but focused on their goal. "Yes, it's fascinating, but let's keep our attention on finding the Astral Lotus." Amber checked the glowing map. "According to this, we should be getting close to the Forest of Luminous Glade." The group made their way to a stunning clearing where the Astral Lotus stood, its petals glowing with an ethereal light. Before they could approach, a voice echoed through the clearing. "To obtain the Petal of the Astral Lotus, you must prove your worth through three trials: the Trial of Courage, the Trial of Wisdom, and the Trial of Unity." The voice seemed to emanate from the forest itself. The adventurers braced themselves for the challenges ahead.

Trial 1: The Trial of Courage

The forest transformed into a landscape filled with their deepest fears.

Violet faced illusions of her favorite magical creatures in peril.

Emerald was surrounded by exaggerated, hostile versions of forest animals.

Amber saw herself failing to solve crucial problems.

Evan confronted monstrous versions of past challenges.

Hounder faced visions of his friends in danger.

Violet stepped forward, trying to overcome her fear. "We can face this together," she said firmly. Emerald, despite her discomfort, pushed through the illusions. "We need to stay focused. These fears are just tricks." Amber used her knowledge to reassure the group. "These are illusions. We know we have the strength to overcome them." Evan, staying resolute, added, "We've handled tough situations before. We can handle this." Hounder, using his quick thinking, helped everyone stay grounded. Together, they faced their fears and proved their courage.

Trial 2: The Trial of Wisdom

The second trial led them into a maze of shimmering walls covered in glowing runes. The maze was a complex puzzle that required careful navigation and problem-solving. Amber studied the map and the runes on the walls. "These runes are a code we need to translate to progress." Emerald, despite her dislike to nature, used her investigative skills to identify hidden clues and avoid magical traps. Violet was excited by the magical characteristics of the maze and presented observations that helped them navigate. Evan, ever the practical thinker, cleared difficulties and made sure they didn't get lost. Hounder used his strategic mind to direct their path and spot any hidden dangers. With their combined efforts and Amber's guidance, they solved the maze's puzzle and reached the final trial.

Trial 3: The Trial of Unity

The final trial was designed to test their unity. The guardian of the lotus appeared, a radiant figure of light. "To earn the Petal of the Astral Lotus, you must demonstrate the strength of your bonds and your unity." Each adventurer shared their true intentions and hopes for their journey.

Violet said, "I want us to succeed and learn more about the magical creatures we encounter."

Emerald expressed, "I hope we achieve our goals efficiently and grow stronger as a team."

Amber added, "I wish for us to gain wisdom and learn from each other's strengths."

Evan shared, "I want us to support each other through every challenge we face."

Hounder spoke, "I believe in our team and want us to stay united and strong."

The guardian's light brightened in response to their heartfelt declarations. "You have shown true unity and understanding. The Petal of the Astral Lotus is yours." With a graceful gesture, the guardian allowed them to take the glowing petal. Violet carefully placed it in the crimson clasp, feeling a rush of accomplishment. As they left the glade, the forest guided them with renewed energy. With the Petal of the Astral Lotus secure, they were one step closer to repairing the Bracelet of Creation. The magical map glowed softly, leading them toward their next destination.

CHAPTER-12
PHOENIX FEATHER OF THE ETERNAL FLAME

"Tip, tip, tip," the rain fell steadily from the heavy, grey sky, creating small puddles that quickly turned into ice. A group of weary travelers huddled beneath a sprawling, ancient tree, its branches barely shielding them from the biting wind that howled through the forest. The air was thickmwith moisture, and each breath they took puffed out in frosty clouds, visible like ghosts dancing in the chill. "It's getting so cold! We need warm clothes, or we'll freeze to death out here!" Amber exclaimed, her voice trembling as she rubbed her arms, trying to generate some warmth against the biting cold that had seeped into their very bones. Hounder nodded, glancing nervously around the fog-shrouded woods. "Winters in Zocadabra are brutal. We can't last long like this." Evan, practical as ever, surveyed the shadowy trees, their outlines blurred by the mist. "Where will we find woollen clothes in a place like this, surrounded by bloodthirsty creatures?" His voice held a hint of panic, eyes darting as if anticipating danger lurking just beyond the veil of fog. Emerald, always the optimist, offered a suggestion. "Let's just wait for the rain to stop. Once it passes, we can make our way to the Phoenix's lair." She had heard whispers of the legendary bird, tales that promised warmth and magic in the heart of winter. "But we're freezing!" Evan's voice shook, and he let out a puff of vapour that vanished into the cold air. Just then, delicate snowflakes began to drift down from the heavy clouds, swirling gracefully as they landed on the ground. "Great, just what we needed. Now we'll definitely become ice statues!" Emerald chuckled softly, unfazed by the falling snow. "I doubt that." With determination, she reached into her satchel and pulled out a shimmering magic charm given to her by the Night Walker. As she cracked it open, a dark blue mist spilled forth, swirling around them like a winter storm. A soft voice echoed from the mist, asking, "What wish do you desire?" Emerald took a deep breath, the cold air sharp in her lungs. "I want you to teleport us to the Phoenix's lair!" She declared, her voice steady despite the chill wrapping around them. In an instant, everything went dark. The sound of the rain faded away, replaced by an eerie silence. When Emerald opened her eyes again, she found herself lying on a warm surface, contrasting sharply with the frost that had clung to her moments before. The air was fragrant and warm, enveloping them like a soft blanket. "Is everyone safe?" Violet called out, her voice breaking the stillness, a faint mist escaping her lips. "Yes!" They all replied, relief washing over them as they adjusted to the new environment. Emerald stood, feeling a rush of wonder as she took in the breath-taking scene. They had arrived in the Phoenix's lair. Emerald looked around, her heart racing with awe. They had arrived in the Phoenix's lair, a cavernous underground realm filled with flowing lava and rivers of molten magma. Glowing cinders floated through the air, illuminating the rough walls of blackened rock, while piles of ash settled in corners, evidence of the Phoenix's fiery existence. The warmth enveloped them like a cosy blanket, a stark contrast to the frigid forest they had just left. The sound of bubbling magma filled their ears, and the ground felt alive beneath their feet, pulsing with heat. "Remember, we're here for the feather," Hounder reminded them, scanning the vast chamber. "It should be in the heart of this lair." Above them, the legendary Phoenix soared gracefully, its brilliant feathers a dazzling array of reds, oranges, and yellows. It circled overhead, leaving trails of sparkling ash in its wake, its presence commanding and majestic. Amber couldn't help but smile, excitement bubbling within her. "We made it!" She exclaimed, her voice filled with wonder as she marvelled at the beauty of the fiery lair. Emerald returned her smile, her heart swelling with hope. "Now, let's find that feather." She felt a spark of magic in the air, a promise of the incredible journey which awaited them ahead. The group moved deeper into the lair, their path illuminated by the glow of molten rock. They navigated around bubbling pools of lava, feeling the heat radiate against their skin. As they ventured further, they could hear the distant echoes of the Phoenix's powerful cry, a sound both beautiful and awe-inspiring. Finally, they reached a massive chamber at the centre of the lair, where the air shimmered with heat and energy. In the middle of the room, surrounded by flickering flames, was the legendary Phoenix, its vibrant feathers glowing like a living fire. Nestled among its fine hair lay the feather of eternal flame, shimmering with an otherworldly light. "Now's our chance," Emerald whispered, her heart pounding in her chest. With a mix of excitement and nervousness, the group prepared to approach the Phoenix, ready to prove their worth and claim the feather that would change their fate forever. As they stood before the majestic Phoenix, the air crackled with energy. Amber stepped forward, her heart pounding. "We seek the feather of eternal flame," she declared, her voice steady. The Phoenix tilted its head, flames dancing in its vibrant plumage. "What makes you worthy of such a gift?" It asked, its gaze piercing through their resolve. Amber took a deep breath. "We need it to make the bracelet of creation which we broke, this is not our first adventure." Just then, a small flash of silver flitted through the air—Silver, their loyal bird, perched gracefully on Amber's shoulder. The Phoenix's eyes widened, a gleam of recognition sparkling within them. "Ah, a silver feathered companion!" It exclaimed, its voice rich with warmth and admiration. "A creature of great beauty and spirit."

Silver chirped happily, his feathers shimmering in the warm glow of the lair. The Phoenix leaned closer, entranced by the bird's elegance. "You are indeed fortunate to travel with such a noble friend. It is a sign of your connection to magic and the natural world." Feeling a rush of pride, Amber smiled at Silver, knowing his presence had brought them good fortune. The Phoenix continued, "Very well, I will consider your request. But to prove your worth, you must each face a challenge." Evan calmly said. " we have faced many, but what is the challenge?" The Phoenix summoned three glowing orbs of light, each pulsing with energy. "Each of you must confront your deepest fear. Only then will the feather reveal itself." Amber nodded, determination filling her. "We had done this before, and we will do it again" "Then step forward," the Phoenix instructed. As they approached the orbs, the world around them began to change. The warmth of the lair faded, and a chilling mist surrounded them, pulling them into their own trials. Amber found herself in a dark forest, eerily similar to the one they had left. Shadows whispered her doubts. "You'll never fix the bracelet," they hissed. Shaking off the chill, she took a deep breath. Remembering her friends and their shared purpose, she said, "I won't give in to fear." With each step, the shadows began to fade, revealing a path forward. Meanwhile, Emerald faced a raging storm, winds howling around her. Memories of their past mistakes flickered like lightning. "You caused this chaos," the storm roared. But with her heart racing, she thought of Amber and the others. "No, we can change this!" She shouted, and the storm began to calm, revealing a clear sky. Evan confronted a vast crater, darkness yawning beneath him. Doubt whispered that he wasn't brave enough to leap across. Yet, he remembered the bond he shared with his companions. "We can do this together," he said, and with that belief, he jumped, soaring into the light. Hounder faced a fearsome creature, a shadow of his insecurities. It growled, towering over him. "You are weak!" It roared. But Hounder stood tall. "I have my friends! Together, we are strong!" He declared, and the creature vanished into a cloud of ash. Violet faces the fear of losing her friends, she found herself alone, but she knew that her friends would never betray her and stood tall against the blankness. As each traveler conquered their fears, they found themselves back in the Phoenix's lair, the air buzzing with anticipation. The Phoenix hovered before them, its feathers glowing brighter than ever. "You have shown true courage. The feather of eternal flame is yours." With a graceful sweep of its wing, the Phoenix summoned the feather, which floated gently toward Violet, shimmering with warmth. She reached out, her fingers brushing its radiant surface, feeling a deep connection to its power. "Use it wisely," the Phoenix advised, its voice filled with ancient wisdom. "Restore what has been broken, and remember, the greatest magic lies in the bonds you share." With gratitude in their hearts, the group thanked the Phoenix. They turned toward the exit, the feather carefully held in Violet's hands—a symbol of hope and a promise of light. Violet then added the last artefact to the crimson clasp, and it started to glow with the brightest light. As they stepped outside, the snow was bright and shined from within. The clasp glowed in response, a beacon of their newfound strength and unity. Silver chirped joyfully, flying high above them, a reminder of the magic that connected them all.

CHAPTER-13
THE BRACELET OF CREATION

The next day, the travellers awoke to a soft snowfall, their skin tingling from frostbite. In Zocadabra, each region had its own distinct weather. The heart of the forest, home to the Zocadabra tribe, was always drenched in warm sunshine. The Phoenix's lair bubbled with intense heat, while the sirens' nesting grounds were cool and humid. The world of giants enjoyed a gentle warmth, all marked clearly on their enchanted map. The area where they stood now was notorious for its extreme temperatures, swinging from icy cold to roasting heat. The map held a magical secret: time flowed differently here. When summer graced one region, winter blanketed another. This land was a mystical patchwork of climates, each more enchanting than the last. Violet, Amber, Emerald,

Evan, Hounder, and Little Silver woke up to the soft glow of morning light, their spirits lifted by the gentle snowfall outside. They gathered together, sharing stories and laughter about their adventures so far, each tale weaving a richer tapestry of the journey. With excitement bubbling in the air, they set their sights on the enchanting land of the fairies. Little Silver, their magical bird, fluttered above them, his shimmering feathers sparkling like stars. The group moved forward, their hearts filled with anticipation for the wonders that awaited them in the fairy realm, where magic danced on every breeze and adventure signed at every turn. Their journey to the fairy realm was quite easy. And there they were, standing at the entrance to the fairy realm. With hearts racing, Violet, Amber, Emerald, Evan, Hounder, and Little Silver exchanged determined glances, ready to seek out Queen Breeze. "Let's go!" Violet urged, leading the way down a winding path adorned with luminescent flowers and twinkling lights. The air was filled with the sweet sounds of laughter and music, drawing them deeper into the enchanting landscape. As they approached the grand palace, a breath-taking structure woven from shimmering branches and adorned with sparkling gemstones, the atmosphere felt charged with magic. Tiny fairies flitted around, their wings glimmering, casting a mixture of colours across the ground. At the entrance, they were met by two regal fairies who bowed gracefully. "Welcome, brave travellers," one of them said, her voice like a soft melody. "You seek Queen of Breeze?" "Yes!" Evan replied, his excitement bubbling over. "We've found the magical items to repair the Bracelet of Creation!" The fairies exchanged knowing glances and stepped aside, allowing the group to enter the palace. Inside, the air shimmered with enchantment, and the walls glowed softly, as if alive with magic. At the centre of the grand hall stood Queen Breeze, radiant and graceful. Her gown flowed like liquid light, and her wings sparkled with every colour of the rainbow. She looked up, her eyes filled with wisdom and warmth. "Welcome, young heroes," Queen Breeze said, her voice resonating like a gentle breeze. "I sense you carry the items needed to mend the Bracelet of Creation." With a nod, the group stepped forward, presenting the Crimson clasp. As they did, a soft glow enveloped the items, responding to the queen's presence. "You have done well to gather these," she said, a smile gracing her lips. "Now, let us restore the magic together." With that, Queen Breeze raised her hands, and the items began to float, swirling in a dance of light. The air crackled with energy as she channelled her magic into them. The Bracelet of Creation shimmered in anticipation, ready to be mended. The travellers held their breath, knowing they were on the brink of restoring balance to their world. Together, they watched as the magic unfolded, their hearts filled with hope and excitement for what was to come. And with a swish and a swash of her hand, the bracelet was mended. "So, you have all the bracelets now?" Asked the queen, her voice tinged with curiosity. "No, but we do have three" said Emerald, just as she did, the chattering, and the tinkling laughs of the tiny fairies transformed into soft gasps and whispers. All of the traveller's eyebrows collected in confusion. "What?" Amber said with a noticeable change in her tone. Breeze said, "don't you know about the reward? "What reward?" Said Evan kind of frustrated as their long journey had just been completed, and another one was starting. "The creator of Zocadabra has kept a reward of one wish for someone who has all the four bracelets, I think you may have a chance, you should go there!" Said Breeze cheerfully. "And WHERE will we find 'THE CREATOR OF ZOCDABRA,' " said Evan, tired, and not at all ready for a ten-thousand miles walk, and a life threatening journey again. "Oh, I can just teleport you there" said Breeze in a fast manner. "Then please do" said Violet in a warm a thanking tone. And just then, everything went… BLUE? (Maybe fairy magic IS blue) Violet opened her eyes to see a tree house, decorated with vines and a cosy warm glow. "I think we are here" said Violet, "Our only way to go back home." "MMHH" Evan replied with a proud nod. An old but lively figure appeared in front of the travellers. "There is no way, G-GRANDFATHER!!!!!!" Said Violet not able to control her amazement. "B-b-but you w-were dead!" Said Emerald in shock. "Oh my dear Emerald, I can never die, I MADE Zocadabra, and it's your duty to save it," said Grandfather while giving the group a trusty look. "Sir, I am Hounder, the prince of the Zocala tribe, we have found three of the bracelets but are not able to find the fourth one," said Hounder, bending one knee and bowing in respect, "I know the reward was for the one who has all the four bracelets but, my friends, they need to go back to their house as soon as possible, and it's my duty to do that, even if I lose my life." "Dear Hounder, stand-up," said grandfather, keeping both of his hands on Hounder's shoulders, "I can give you the wish right now, but that would mean that this group of young children are disrespecting their duties." "And we wouldn't do that, will we?" Amber said stepping forward, holding Hounder's hand with a tight but assuring grip. "Bring on the challenge," said Evan holding Amber's hand. "Together we can achieve anything," said Emerald holding Evans hand. "We will find the fourth bracelet," said Violet gripping onto Emerald's hand. "I am impressed by your unity...... I do have a clue for you," said grandfather with a playful smirk on his face. "But remember, this is going to be the toughest challenge you are going to ever face, you will find out things that will break and chatter you to your core, are you willing to take up the challenge?" "WE ARE!" The whole group stated. "Well then, here is the clue" said Violet's grandfather piercing into the group's eyes;

"The fourth bracelet I have in my grasp,
Darkness, that's my past.

Wise I may be, but books are my call,
a leaf tattoo on my wrist tells all.

No wife I have, my intentions are dark,
someone the girls know well, yet miss the mark.
Who am I, can you tell?

I am someone who can turn your life into a hell.

My face must be sweet, but I have a shadow within,

As for you all, THE JOURNEY BEGINS."

END OF BOOK ONE

www.ingramcontent.com/pod-product-compliance
Lightning Source LLC
LaVergne TN
LVHW041851070526
838199LV00045BB/1552